2

A Project Named Desire

BY JOHN WILLIAM CORRINGTON AND JOYCE H. CORRINGTON

So Small a Carnival
A Project Named Desire

ALSO BY JOHN WILLIAM CORRINGTON

POETRY
Where We Are
Mr. Clean and Other Poems
The Anatomy of Love
Lines to the South

FICTION
And Wait for the Night
The Upper Hand
The Lonesome Traveller and Other Stories
The Bombardier
The Actes and Monuments
The Southern Reporter
Shad Sentell

EDITED WITH MILLER WILLIAMS
Southern Writing in the Sixties: Fiction
Southern Writing in the Sixties: Poetry

A Project
Named Desire

———

John William Corrington
Joyce H. Corrington

Viking

VIKING
Viking Penguin Inc., 40 West 23rd Street,
New York, New York 10010, U.S.A.
Penguin Books Ltd, Harmondsworth,
Middlesex, England
Penguin Books Australia Ltd, Ringwood,
Victoria, Australia
Penguin Books Canada Limited, 2801 John Street,
Markham, Ontario, Canada L3R 1B4
Penguin Books (N.Z.) Ltd, 182–190 Wairau Road,
Auckland 10, New Zealand

First published in 1987 by Viking Penguin Inc.
Published simultaneously in Canada

LIBRARY OF CONGRESS CATALOGING IN PUBLICATION DATA
Corrington, John William.
A project named Desire.
I. Corrington, Joyce H.   II. Title.
PS3553.07P76 1987   813'.54   86-9093
ISBN 0-670-81192-0

Printed in the United States of America by
R. R. Donnelley & Sons Company,
Harrisonburg, Virginia
Set in Palatino
Design by Lucy Albanese

A. M. D. G.

And for Lee Audrey George
and
Ossie Hawkins—

*Friends without whom the journey
of this life would have been much
harder and less filled with love and
friendship.*

*Thy waste and thy desolate places
and the land of thy destruction
shall even now be too narrow by
reason of the inhabitants, and
the children thou shalt have
after thy barrenness shall say
again in thy ears: The place is too
strait for me. Give place to me
that I may dwell.*

—ISAIAH 49:19–20

A Project
Named Desire

CHAPTER
1

I left New Orleans before dawn, using the River Road and some funny little shunts this way and that on dirt and gravel sidetracks to make sure I was going to be all by myself when I reached the Bon Chance Motel just off the LSU campus in Baton Rouge.

As I turned onto the old Airline Highway, I pulled off the road and lit myself a cigar, watching everything that passed me. Nothing came by but an old man in a pickup truck and two ladies in a mint red-and-white 1957 Chevy. No light planes or choppers up above. Just cool October air and me in my black Olds sitting under a liveoak tree that seemed about the same age as the land itself.

I was ahead of schedule. I watched the smoke of my Marsh-Wheeling curl up against the windshield and thought about how I'd managed to bring the whole thing this far.

An old cop I used to work with years ago, Sergeant Francis Murray, gave me the bottom line about moving witnesses: *if nobody knows but you, nobody shows but you.*

That's the way I was handling Peetie Postum. I was

picking up Peetie to take him to Orleans Parish Criminal Court, Section K, to testify in *State* v. *Franco Xavier Burnucci*, a/k/a Mr. X.

That's what the old timers called Burnucci on the street. In a very low voice. With great respect.

Word was he'd been running the action in New Orleans and the parishes hereabouts for forty years. His folks had brought him to the New World when he was nine or ten, and five years later he'd made his bones and started his run for the end of the road and the top of the heap. He was over seventy now, and he had it all in the round of his hand. Numbers, whores, dope, sports fixes. If they wouldn't sell it or do it on the street, you went to Burnucci.

Still, ordinarily Burnucci wouldn't have meant anything to me. I'm a captain of Homicide in the New Orleans Police Department. I don't give a damn what you do unless you pull somebody's chain so hard it breaks off.

But lately I'd gotten interested in Mr. X. Drug dealers had begun falling away like autumn leaves. The local dope world had lost two of its stars in the last six weeks and three more were missing.

Everybody knew what was happening, but Our Noble System of Law doesn't give a shit about what everybody knows. Maybe that's what's wrong. Blind justice? How about deaf, dumb, and riddled with the clap, too? The bitch can't seem to do right.

What was happening made you think of the old days. When they were what they call consolidating in the oil business, running all the little folks out. Drugs are just another commodity, and the rap on the streets was that Burnucci had gone to popping the independents. Waste the competition and hike the price. Like old H. Rap used to say, it's as American as cherry pie.

I knew what was going down and where the orders

were coming from when we found Murphy Dunkle with his throat cut sitting on a toilet at the Sheraton and fished Wee-Wee Harris from the river with both his eyes blown out. I could have painted you a picture. But I needed somebody to fill in the numbers for me. No sweat. I'm good at that.

If I got paid for what I do in the office, it'd be public corruption. But things balance out because they can't pay me enough for street duty. Nobody knows what Rat Trapp knows. See, I got the power to cloud men's minds. With the threat of five to ten, twenty to life. Folks talk to me. Most of the time I can clear a homicide in a day or two just walking around in the housing projects and neighborhoods, being seen, listening.

But nobody wanted to talk about my two dopers and how they got themselves lost. You put the mouth on Burnucci, and Shongaloo ain't far enough away. His folks will track your ass down in Marrakech or up in Oslo, and they'll do you. They'll do you something terrible.

Ah, but there's exceptions to everything. Never mind who, but one evening at the Kit-Kat Klub, somebody passing by my table fast whispered to me, Peetie Postum. Of course. Why not? That miserable sonofabitch.

Peetie was not a nice person. Fact, the best day of his life, Peetie would have scared a Russian tank. Near seven feet, 340 pounds. Almost made the NFL, but in his last college game, at Grambling, something ticked him off and he broke his defensive coach's arm. After that, he was just meat for hire. I'd been wondering what Peetie did to feed that frame. But Peetie had been careful. He knew all he had to do was cough hard and I'd be staring down his throat—with a .357 Magnum for a tongue depressor.

Once I'd heard that whisper, the rest was easy. I hit his little place on Tonti Street with a warrant about seven o'clock one morning when Peetie was just going to bed.

He come around like a lamb when I tucked the barrel of my piece into his eye, and, sure enough, in a back closet we found all kinds of crap.

Never mind the nose candy and kif—which was very good stuff. In amongst the potsherds and idols, I found a packet of traveler's checks signed by Murphy Dunkle. And a Rolex watch, and a carat-and-a-half diamond ring Wee-Wee Harris had bought in happier days at Mexic Brothers on Canal Street. And a .22 Magnum with slugs that I knew were lead brothers to the ones they lifted out of Wee-Wee's eyesockets. Game, set, and match, as Denise Lemoyne, my pal in the DA's office, would say. Me? I don't play tennis. I play grab-ass.

Peetie knew what I knew, and he didn't have no objection to being taken for a breakfast and a nice long talk. Louisiana's started burning its trash again, and Peetie had them special circumstances that set you down in the charged chair printed all over his record.

I've had better breakfasts, and I've had worse, but Peetie talked like a sports announcer trying to fill a slow ball game. Did he implicate? Oh, didn't it rain? Yes, good people. Peetie pissed all over his employer, drank five beers, and went to pissing again. He made Burnucci on both the killings over a dozen eggs and two pounds of bacon—after his wake-up beers.

So I had Peetie Postum on tape and in the flesh ready to put the hex on Mr. X. All I needed was one more thing to make a package. I told Peetie what I wanted.

—Man, you fullashit.

—Yeah, I know. Watch it don't fall on you.

—Man, I go wired to Burnucci, they gonna pat me down and turn me off. Send your stereo.

—He still owes you for Wee-Wee and Murphy, right?

—Yeah. But he'll send it around.

—You ain't gonna *be* around.

—I ain't goin' wired neither. Why you think I'm talkin' to you? 'Cause I want to be dead? Shit, that's easy.

I could see Peetie's point. He wasn't one of Burnucci's regular people. He was contracted labor. They'd feel him up just the way he was saying. But I needed Burnucci paying off. I was gonna *have* Burnucci paying off. I got to thinking.

When it come to me, I just smiled. It was so good I could hardly believe it.

See, Burnucci owned plenty of straight stuff, too. All kinds of real estate that was slums just then, but rotting and moldering on the edge of the central business district where some hotel chain or oil company or insurance outfit was sooner or later gonna cut off a hand and pass it to him just for the ground underneath his tenements. And he owned a couple of clubs in the Quarter that his son, Nick, ran for him.

Lately Mr. X had been doing a lot of business at one of Nick's places, the Vegas East. The old man liked to watch the girls strip. He liked having a table of his own in back where people could come by and ask favors and pay respect. He'd paid his dues. Why not a little fun and games down in the Quarter?

I'll tell you why not. The old man must have thought his kid had brains enough not to let his place get rigged for sound, but he was wrong. Nick Burnucci was very mean but never swift.

The feds and NOPD Narcotics had one of the Vegas East busboys wired. Not that Raphael liked carrying cable, but they had him made on possession with intent, and since he was as cute as a college coed, he reckoned taking his chances with Mr. X wasn't any worse than taking what they were gonna stick to him in the state prison at Angola. Smart boy.

Tyndall in Narcotics had told me that for weeks all they

had been getting on the wire was bullshit. They got tapes they could sell to a gourmet newspaper column. The old man talking minestrone, talking tortellini, ravioli. He's telling people about a little place in Milano does the finest fettuccine in the world. He's going on about how Italian wine has more character than French. You want to know about Lacrima Christi? They got forty minutes on tape about volcanic soil, temperature, climate. It's good they got tape. Nobody could stay awake to take that crap down shorthand.

My idea was to give Burnucci something more interesting to talk about. But I knew better than to try to get a hand from Tyndall and the feds. If Hitler come back pushing dope, those dumb bastards would fight off the Israeli secret service to make him for a kilo of coke. See, we're talking quota and jurisdiction and media coverage, which is to say agency and department budget and... you don't want to hear this shit. So I called in to Central Lockup and got hold of Maxine Hawkins, this sweet chocolate dish who'd come over to Homicide from Vice a couple of months ago.

—Max, you still got a line to the narcs?

—Sure, Captain. Vice and the narcs are two hands shaking each other.

—I wouldn't touch either one. I need a frequency. What do they use for a remote transmitter?

She was quiet for a minute. —Anything special?

—Naw. Just an idea for down the line is all.

—You want me to call you where you are?

—I'm moving around. I'll get back in an hour.

Make that two hours. That's when Peetie walked through the door of Vegas East, clean as he could be. Just dropping by to pick up some walking around money.

Me? I'm two doors down in my car with a receiver and

a tape machine, right next to the fed's stakeout in back of the T-shirt shop next to Vegas East. When Peetie eases in and goes to chow down with Mr. X, the feds don't know *I'm* taping them taping Raphael taping Burnucci.

The old man is telling him they shouldn't be meeting like this, and Peetie is saying it's cool. He just wants his pay for Wee-Wee and Murphy, and to know if Mr. X has got any other street work? Then, would you believe it, Burnucci goes to talking about some other dealers who've given him trouble over the years. Does Peetie know 'em? Sure he does. Okay, you done good on Harris and Murphy, whatever his name. These other guys. Lose 'em, Burnucci tells him. They been pressing my man at Desire. He's a good nigger. I got to look out for him. You gimme a deal on four? Peetie is sitting there eating. Then, with his mouth full, he says, Okay, you're a good customer. I need five big ones for four. Finish your lunch, Mr. X tells him. You want any more, just ask.

The rest of it was chewing and swallowing, and it went on a long time, but I had Mr. X right where the left diagonal crosses the right. The feds would give their buzzard scout badge with the bronze fruit leaf to get my tape and send me to Wyoming. Too late. I'm riding their frequency, and their warrant. And I'm in the DA's office with Assistant DA Denise Lemoyne before they can figure out who walked away with their nuts in a sack.

Skip the rest of it. The indictments went down just like Wee-Wee and Murphy had. Burnucci is going insane, screaming about the *schwartzers*, about his son, Nick, who lets his old man get made in his own club hiring faggot waiters.

But Burnucci is in control compared to the feds and NOPD Narcotics. They tried to get a federal judge to quash the state indictments. They tried to get my badge pulled. Madness, threats, racial slurs, promises of non-cooperation for a thousand years. That's okay. Homicide 1, Fed-Narcs zip.

Now it was time to sew the thing up. We'd kept Peetie out of the parish for almost six months, and this particular morning he was coming in to do *La Forza del Destino* in front of an Orleans Parish criminal jury.

I started the car again and pulled on to Airline Highway. If somebody was following me, he'd stolen Stealth technology. The cars on the road were what they ought to be, and my Olds blended in just fine.

I remember how good I felt. The sun was up by then, and you could see ten miles. The breeze was cool, but not cold. Call it Indian summer. It made me wish I had more time to spend outside fishing and hunting. In the country. In daylight. Tough. It ain't ever gonna be. I fish and hunt at night. In the city. You say you got a ten-pound bass last week, and eight doves? I got a 210-pound killer and a whole town full of canaries.

Bon Chance looked all right. No cars parked with anyone inside. Nobody checking in or out. I went around to the room in the back. Len Dalton and Bob Girot were in there trying to get Peetie to stop eating. Peetie had gone to fat waiting for that day. He must have weighed 420 pounds, and Bob was saying as how, with Peetie in the car, we couldn't outrun a ten-speed bike.

—This is gonna be a nice quiet ride. Right, Peetie?

—Ri . . .

—Youall ready?

They looked strung out, hanging on the wire over a pit they couldn't see. I had to get them calmed down.

—All we got to do is walk maybe a hundred yards and drive eighty miles. You boys know how to walk, don't you? Leave the driving to me.

They tried to laugh, but it didn't work. They were good

boys, but they knew what kind of money must be out for a hit on Peetie. We'd heard it was six figures. An open contract. Take him out and pick it up.

That meant if our security went down, they'd be lined up along the highway like it was deer season opening. It was anybody's money. All the hoods in South Louisiana had been cleaning their guns and asking questions for six months. It ain't Chicago in 1930, but we've got some bad asses down here.

We put body armor on Peetie—at least we tried. Nothing really fit, so we kind of lapped three or four jackets around him and held them in place with friction tape. He looked like a big black package you wouldn't want to get from UPS.

Len and Bob had AR-15s. I had just brought along my Colt Cobra .357 with a 5½-inch barrel. I thought if it got worse than that, we'd be better off running than standing anyhow.

We came out of the room and walked along a covered area that led toward the parking lot. There were flower-boxes and ice machines and cold-drink dispensers along the way, and we knew to move from one shelter to the next. Until we hit the last sixty yards or so. It was open concrete sidewalk running past the pool, with the morning sun playing down on it, sparkling off the water. No way to get the car closer.

I led the way, watching, looking back, noticing the smell of late flowers and chlorine from the pool, thinking, *Okay, a couple dozen yards, then you're on the road, and . . .*

We never quite made it to the road. We didn't even make the car.

The first .30–.30 round drove splinters of concrete into my leg. The second one dropped Len like an invisible eighteen-wheeler had just brushed past him. I turned and turned, trying to see where the hell the shooting was coming from.

Then I looked east, over one wing of the motel. The sun looked like it was camped up on the second-story roof, and even with sunglasses I couldn't see a thing. I pointed up there, and Bob let go with his automatic rifle, but the .30–.30 rounds just kept coming. Peetie stood there frozen, looking up at the rising sun above the roof as if he'd expected it all the time, as if it would be a waste of energy to try to get out of range. I yelled to Peetie to run, but just as he turned I saw all four-hundred pounds of him picked up, pushed through the air for three or four yards, and dropped at the edge of the pool.

I managed to drag Len over by the flowerboxes and then sprinted back toward Peetie—whether I could move him or not. The shot must have hurt him, but with all that body armor and muscle and fat on him, at that range, it hadn't necessarily penetrated.

I almost reached him before the last shot sounded. I was maybe six feet from Peetie when the final .30–.30 hit him square in the face. It was like watching a huge rosebud open at super-speed, and open and open. Till the red liquid petals splashed off my jacket, off my hands, my cheeks.

—Oh, shit, I yelled, knowing it was over, turning and starting to fire up at the empty roof, into the enormous red sun, as if I could bring it down with a well-placed shot.

When only silence answered my shots, I sat down on the cool cement beside Peetie and watched all that blood running over the rim of the pool, into the clear shimmering water. Bob came over, put his hand on my shoulder. Then, with the barrel of his rifle, he picked up something lying near Peetie's hand. It was a big jelly-filled donut. With one bite gone.

CHAPTER

2

When the Baton Rouge police got done, I headed back for New Orleans. Len had to stay overnight in the hospital, but Bob drove back with me.

The Baton Rouge people had been very nice. Nobody said, Why the hell do you New Orleans types let that toilet you call a city overflow, spew out all over the rest of the state? No, they went over the motel carefully, checked out witnesses all around the neighborhood. So that before we started back down the I-10 we knew for certain what we had known from the start. A very professional job. No brass casings left around, no prints, no vehicle spotted, nobody seen running. A lot of unanswered questions. Uppermost in my mind: how had I fucked up and let them find Peetie? But no answers.

Just as a door opened, a door closed. And Peetie Postum going home later in a packing crate one of the local trucking firms nailed together for a reasonable price when the East Baton Rouge Parish coroner found out they don't make coffins quite that big.

I dropped Bob at Central Lockup on Tulane and Broad

streets to try to explain what had happened to our boss, Major Mauvais, while I headed for the courtroom where Burnucci's hearing was under way.

New Orleans has a city hall that looks like a criminal court building, and, of course, a criminal court building that looks like city hall. When you come to think of it, that's all right. What with the way Louisiana politics goes, some folks would say a better class of people turns up at criminal court.

Even inside it's not your average municipal building. You could have a football scrimmage in the front hallway. Be a great set for a movie chase. Somebody brings in a weapon, passes it to a con, and away we go. Big vaulted Art Deco ceiling, sweeping stairways, marble floors. Nobody ever did tell me why they spent so much on a place where there's never a damned thing going on but misery.

While the Baton Rouge police were doing their thing, I'd phoned the Orleans Parish DA's office and filled them in on what had happened. Denise Lemoyne had seemed almost stoic about it. As if she and Peetie had shared the same opinion. Shit, maybe everybody was right but me. A long time ago, Sergeant Murray told me, *You don't put a million bucks in jail. You just don't.* Inflation had raised the numbers, but the principle was the same. Maybe trying to cage Burnucci was like shooting at the sun. They'd have to prove it to me. I wasn't convinced.

I was almost to the Division K courtroom when I saw a knot of people gathered outside, and a medical team come barreling out of the courtroom with a gurney. I started to reach for my iron, thinking my scenario, my chase scene, had already started. It was Judge Starke's courtroom. Maybe he'd taken one. Maybe I didn't care. I never had liked the way Starke read his lawbooks.

Then I saw Nick Burnucci and his cousin, Kenny Amadeo, in amongst the medics. When I looked down at the face on the gurney, there was Nick's dear old dad, Mr. X, looking gray and wasted and very tired. Even at that, he looked better than Peetie.

—Where you taking him?

—Sacre Coeur, one of the medics replied. That was the big expensive hospital that catered to rich locals and Latin millionaires who came Stateside for their medical care.

—What the fuck? What's going down?

Wes Colvin, a reporter for the *Item* and one of the best friends I've got, said in my ear,—I think your whole case. In flames. Starke just gave Burnucci an indefinite continuance. Health reasons.

—You're shitting me.

—What you see is what he got. Amadeo's a sharp lawyer. If you'd heard the expert medical testimony...

Wes and I stood there looking with our eyeballs hanging out while they pushed Burnucci past us.

—Goddamn, I said. —They're paying off that little bastard in the judge suit.

Wes shrugged. —You want an argument, you're gonna have to find somebody else to have it with.

Amadeo heard us. He stopped as the ambulance people pushed on by. He was the *consigliere* for the Burnucci family and looked like a cross between a Brooks Brothers salesman and a dago waiter.

—That's bad talk, Captain Trapp. Maybe you better save it for the neighborhood bars.

—Maybe I ought to break your cheekbones, Counselor. One of these days...

—I've heard your name mentioned in local political circles, Captain, but I can't see you with a future there. You're not sensitive... to civil rights.

I reached for him as he walked on, but Wes pulled down my arm. We stood there watching Nick Burnucci and Amadeo looking concerned, Franco Xavier looking half-dead, and the medics looking bored as the whole parade vanished down the long marble hallway. I been to Hollywood, I been to Redwood, but this one was too much for me. It crossed my mind that even with Peetie alive they'd still be pushing Franco right out the door.

Just then, Denise Lemoyne came stalking out of the courtroom. She was the assistant DA on Burnucci's case, and Wes's lady. Wes started to say something to her.

—Don't, she said, a little crackle in her voice. —Please don't say anything. Damn that creepy excuse for a judge . . .

Wes and I stood there. If I didn't like Burnucci's getting a continuance, it creased Denise real bad. This was her first heavy case since she'd joined the DA's staff. She and I had spent hours setting it up note by note. We'd prepped Peetie together. She could play the whole piece from memory. She didn't even need that satchel of papers she was carrying to try it. Now, in the space of a couple of hours, she'd gotten all the bad news a prosecutor could handle.

After a minute or two, she managed a weak smile.

—Thank you for your consideration, gentlemen. Then Denise reached up and hugged me, looking me over for holes. —You all right, Rat?

—I'm fine. Len Dalton took a .30–.30 through the meat of his leg, but he'll be okay, too.

—Poor Peetie, she said.

—Don't sweat Peetie, I told her. —About now, he's explaining to Murphy and Wee-Wee how come he came up early.

—Up? Wes asked with a grin.

—I meant down. If I look like crying, it's for the case.

—Ah, the case, Denise said bitterly. —I think you can slam-dunk the case, boys. Amadeo had three doctors dancing, two cardiologists crowing . . .

—And you guys lost your partridge, Peetie Postum, Wes finished.

—I'm not sure it matters, Denise said. —Starke's continuance could hold for the next five years.

—You think it's righteous? I asked.

She frowned and shrugged. —What do I know? The state can't pay doctors like Burnucci does.

Then her face cleared, and she smiled at us. —Let's try to forget it over a drink. How about lunch at that little bistro in the Quarter with triple-size martinis?

—The service is too slow, Wes said. —I've got to be at the Desire housing project by one o'clock.

We both stared at him. —You know something I don't? I asked him. Nobody goes to the Desire project if they don't have to.

—There's an anti-drug rally I've got to cover for the *Item*, he said.

—You got to be kidding, I said. —The goddamn place invented T's and blues. They turn more doses in there than...

Wes laughed. —You ever hear of a rock band with the same name?

Denise looked like she had. —Desire Project? That's the band that made the hit record...

—... "Wise Child," Wes nodded. —Platinum in nine weeks. A very big outfit right now. It seems there's New Orleans connections. The lead singer's from here.

I laughed. —So they're gonna play against dope in the projects. What do you bet dope wins?

Denise frowned. —Come on, Rat. You do what you can. All of us do. Anyhow, I heard that in Philadelphia they set up a hot-line for calls about dealers, and got information that led to some indictments.

—Where do youall want to eat? I asked.

—Desire Project is playing at the Superdome tonight, isn't it? Denise asked Wes.

—Yeah, Wes replied. —And I've got press passes. I'd thought you'd be tied up with the trial, but now...

—Eats, anyone? I said again. —How about Sally Marshall's?

But Denise had brightened and was telling Wes,—I'd love to go. Maybe it's just arrested development, but when Danny Bynum sings...

—Danny Bynum? I asked, and felt an old-time shiver moving up my spine.

Sally Marshall's restaurant, a few blocks back of the Pontchartrain Hotel on Baronne Street, was full up with the lunch crowd and hot as a doper's spoon. The ceiling fans didn't help. They just stirred the heat, mixed in the odors of cooking food that drifted out from the kitchen, and left us all sweating just the way we would have been if they were off.

Sally's is a black restaurant. Not that she discourages white folks. Sally's been around. She can stand anybody so long as they don't talk loud, drink too much, take to throwing food or throwing up. I never found Sally's house rules confining.

Wes and I ate there once or twice a week. We always had something to talk about, what with me running Homicide and him doing mainly the police beat for the *Item*. Sally served our kind of food. Creole Southern. Chicken necks and pig's feet, oxtails and dirty rice, neck bones, gizzards, and banana fritters.

That day the special was fried perch, hush puppies, stuffed eggplant, and a nice squirrel gumbo to start.

Two of the items were illegal. You can't sell game fish or squirrels, but Sally didn't give a damn. She had people out in the parishes who made a living poaching for her, and the customers just ate, drank, paid, and smiled.

But I could see right off that it was all new to Denise. She's a fine woman from what passes for good family in Uptown New Orleans. But Sally Marshall's place wouldn't be the first restaurant her crowd thought of if somebody lisped, Luncheon, anyone? She had a fine high-born smile pasted on her face as she looked the place over. Could be she was seeing people she'd be prosecuting one day soon. For all I knew, she'd never been in a room full of blacks before. Wes looked over at me and winked.

—Uh, is there a menu? Denise asked in a small voice.

—Sure, Wes answered.

He pointed through the steam and haze at a big blackboard on the back wall.

—That's it over there.

Denise smiled. —Continental style, she said brightly.

—Yeah, Wes said. —Is that so?

—Well, I mean . . . Denise's voice trailed off.

I wasn't taking much part in the repartee. Even before we ordered, I had plenty to digest.

—I'm going with the neck bones, Wes said, squinting at the blackboard. —And the dirty rice.

—Neck . . . bones, Denise echoed.

—You always do, I told Wes. —If you'd try the pig-feet, you'd never trot back.

—Pig . . . feet, Denise said weakly. —I don't think I . . .

—I had me a fatback omelet once, Wes said, winking at me to hold up my end of the put-on. —Fried skins on the side, field peas, and grits.

We could see Denise hadn't yet heard a dish she recognized as fit for human consumption.

—You both . . . eat things like that?

Wes smiled. —See, baby, Rat's black—you must have noticed—and I'm your upstate country redneck. We was poor kids together. In different places.

Denise tried to smile back. —Do you suppose there might be blackened redfish?

Wes and I exchanged a startled look.

—Maybe fish-head chowder, I said. —But you see, us poor folks never got a whole fish. Our tastes got shaped by poverty.

—Right, Wes came back, looking somber. —Where we ate when we were growing up, the big restaurants dumped their garbage. Then cooks like Sally picked through it and tried to do what they could.

It was nice, the way he did it. For just a second, you could see that Denise was wondering. That one second of doubt was the price she paid for her money, private schools, and a life lived off at a tangent from the rest of us. But it passed quick. She gave both of us a mean look.

—I'll have the oxtails, she said firmly. —Unless they have horse entrails.

We both grinned. —That's Thursday, Wes said. —We can come back then if you want.

The three of us drank Dixie beer and jabbered about Burnucci's continuance till the food came. Then, as I fell silent eating, Denise looked over at me. Maybe you could call her expression sly.

—Rat, when are you going to tell us about Danny Bynum?

I just kept eating.

—I don't believe he is, Wes drawled. —I mean, what with Desire Project being a major band and all...Rat doesn't name-drop. It's not kosher. I mean, couth.

Denise spit out a piece of oxtail gristle in the most delicate way and gave Wes a withering look.

—I don't think Rat heard the question. He was up to his ears in...whatever that is he's eating.

—I heard. I've been thinking on it since we left court.

Wes stared at me in mock seriousness. —It's a story, right?

—Wrong. Out of sight. Out of mind. Off the record.

But that didn't end it. They both looked like kids hoping for the kind of fairy tale that grown folks tell 'em just before they go off to sleep to dream their own.

—Long time ago, I said slowly,—there was this girl, Camille Bynum. Beautiful, smart, lots of everything. The two of us lived in the Desire project. Hell, we were both born there. She was as close as you could get to the girl next door. Two courts down, second building, upstairs apartment in the west corner. By the time we were twenty, we'd known each other...twenty years. Most of it together, a lot of it loving time.

Denise and Wes were hooked. Not by the story, but because it came from me. Seems I generate an image that goes with lost lives, not lost loves.

—This was 'sixty-five, and the Movement was in high gear. Black dudes walking around with one hand on a knife or a pistol and the other one on their crotch. Everybody thinking it was just two weeks and another demonstration till they moved out to Lakeside or into the Garden District.

—I do remember, Wes said. —All us good old boys moving at night with shotguns in our cars. Looked like we were all gonna get it on, didn't it?

—Camille was real light-skinned, I said. —Back then, you wouldn't believe how much that mattered. Now and again, she'd tell me how she could pass for white if she picked up and left town. Just go to L.A., she said, and it'd be a whole new world.

—That broke you up? Denise asked.

—Hell, I don't know. I had me a job driving a truck for old man D'Annunzio, the seafood dealer. I was talking getting married to Camille. She loved me, but I think she saw us married as a life sentence to the projects. She could handle most things, but she couldn't handle that. Said they'd just opened the freedom road, and she was gonna get herself a ticket to ride.

—Everyone wants to move up, don't they? Denise asked innocently.

—Yeah, I said, coming back out of a sadness twenty years old. —Unless they get born as far Uptown as you can get.

Wes and Denise both looked at me in surprise.

—Sorry, I said. —See, I was just feeling my story. You got to understand that if you live in the projects, Up is Out. One day I come home smelling of crawfish and crabs, and Camille's momma told me she'd gone off with some white man. He'd come in a big white Cadillac car, with a couple of other guys just to keep the brothers cool, and took her off. Last thing she did was hand her momma five hundred-dollar bills and say, "'Bye, Momma. I'm on my way. You tell Ralph I'll see him on down the road."

We all sat quiet for a minute or so. Me remembering how I felt that damned hot August day, Denise and Wes respecting it.

—So the next day I went down and signed up army. It was that or get myself killed looking for that white bastard who took her off without even her clothes or anything else. Just took her like you reach in a pen in a pet shop and take away a puppy you like. Money talks. Bullshit walks.

—Military instead of militant, Wes mused.

I did the best grin I could. —I keep telling you, you got a way with words. You ought to try writing.

—Little bitty talent, he said. —I'd end up on a crummy newspaper. Better I stay in Big Oil.

Denise wasn't smiling. She was looking at me with this tender sad expression.

—You've never forgotten, have you?

I shook my head. —I carried Camille Bynum through Basic and Advanced. She was fooling around in my head all the time I was in Military Police School. She went to Germany with me.

Denise reached out impulsively, touched my hand. —You still love her, don't you? That's why you've never married.

Wes and I looked at each other, then at her.

—Shit, Wes said in mild amazement,—who's telling the story?

Denise stared right back at him. —I know what I know.

Wes laughed out loud. —Baloney. He forgot her in a whorehouse in Germany, came home older and wiser.

—He did not. He's never forgotten her. Look at him. Can't you hear it in his voice? Is that why you never married, Rat?

—He never married because he found out it's no use buying a cow when you can milk it through the fence.

That set Denise off. She half rose from the table, looking really mad. Denise and Wes were engaged but had put off marrying because of recent deaths in her family. I wondered if my buddy's smart mouth had just cost him more than he wanted to pay.

—If that's what you think of marriage...

Wes looked hurt, innocent. —Hell, baby, that's not what I think. It's what Rat thinks.

Denise broke up laughing, sat down, and shook her head.

—There's got to be a better crowd for me to run with, she said.

—Not if you stay in the DA's office, I laughed back. —Believe it or not, you're sitting with the crème de la crème right now.

Wes was quiet for a minute. I thought maybe that last

shot of Denise's had tenderized him a little. But no, he was thinking.

—One thing about your story, he said. —What makes you connect your Camille Bynum with this kid who fronts Desire Project?

—I was in Germany, I said. —We were doing some tight stuff with East German dissidents, trying to bring people out over the Wall. I got this one letter from Camille. She said she had a little boy named Danny, and she was happy. She wished me all the best, said I deserved it. A while back, I saw the kid on some TV track. It was like looking at his mother.

—Oh, God, Denise breathed. —Love is . . . so long.

—It was for me, I told her. —Love . . . and then, so long. But if she's happy . . .

Denise grabbed my arm like she meant to take it with her. —Wes has press tickets to the concert. Come with us. Please.

I reached across and kissed her on the cheek.

—Listen, you two don't never want to quarrel. You want to hold on to what you've got.

—Hello, young lovers, Wes sang in a quavering voice, and Denise elbowed him into silence. I managed a laugh.

—Youall go on, I told Denise. —Halfass here is due out at the project, where they might just gonna eat him alive. And you got to go defend truth and justice.

—How about it, Rat? Denise persisted. —It would be fun to go to the concert together. Forget what happened today.

—No, I said. —Twenty years is a long time.

—But not long enough?

—Yeah, I told her. —It's long enough. A lot of people don't even live that long. Anyhow, I've got other stuff on my mind. Like finding who pulled the trigger on Peetie Postum.

CHAPTER

3

When I got back to the office, Maxine Hawkins was waiting for me.

—I hear Peetie's history, she said. —What happened?

Max had done some of the babysitting with Peetie in Baton Rouge, so she had a right to ask. I had to tell her that somehow I'd fucked up. Despite all my secret agent moves, I must have carried the button man to the Bon Chance.

—So what's left of the Burnucci case? Max asked.

Without Peetie, all we had was tapes and a video deposition. That wouldn't do it. You can't cross-examine either one. —Burnucci's lawyer got him a continuance. Now he'll go in and ask for dismissal. And that little pimp Starke will smile and give it to him.

After that I sat at my desk feeling sorry for myself. I believe I still had the long-time old-days broken-hearted blues left over from lunch. When I stopped thinking about Peetie and the Burnucci case, I got to thinking about Camille. *Trapp*, I said to myself, *let it go. It's been gone so long you're not even feeling it. You're just feeling your age. What you need is to spend time with a new woman, get your mind off killing and the old days.*

Just then, Max came back in carrying an envelope.

—This just came in by messenger, Captain. How much do you pay your stoolies, anyhow?

I laughed and studied Maxine. Even in a cop suit, she looked very good indeed. Milk-chocolate skin, short fluffy hair, lips that could take the pain away. I'd worked with her when she first came out of the academy. She'd been my driver for a few months before she went over to Vice. But good things don't last, and I'd been too busy just then to take advantage while it did. Anyhow, Max had kept to herself. People told me she didn't spend much off-duty time with other cops. But then maybe the right cop hadn't asked.

—Sergeant...

—Sir?

—With Peetie gone, you won't be going back to Baton Rouge. What have you got on for tonight?

—Just what you're looking at, Captain. I volunteered for off-duty security at the Superdome.

—Some rock concert.

—*The* rock concert. You ever hear Danny Bynum and Desire Project?

—Yeah. Hell of a name, don't you think?

—What can I tell you? When that boy sings, it's heaven.

—When you get back down to earth, I want to feed you.

Maxine smiled. Whether a woman's interested or not, it always spikes her feelings when a man says something like that.

—Just say when and where, Captain.

—Catch you tomorrow, precious thing... I mean, Sergeant.

She walked out with a little more swing than what she

brought in. The child had a fine hindsight. I hated to see her leave, but it was nice to watch her walk away.

I opened the envelope. Inside was one of those flyers they hand out in the neighborhoods for gospel singers and folks like B. B. King. This one was for Desire Project. With it was a box-seat ticket. I smiled, thinking, Denise Lemoyne won't let go when she's got the scent. That story of mine had caught hold of her. Tough old cop with a twenty-year secret sorrow. I almost laughed, but not quite. Then I dropped the flyer and the ticket in the wastebasket next to my desk.

Once, a long time ago, when I was first working the street, I pulled security where they were digging up an old cemetery, moving the graves for a new high-rise building. Some of the coffins broke open, and I saw up close what the past looks like when you go to rooting in it. I'd let the concert go on by. Good luck to Camille, good luck to her little boy who'd taken the name of a hellhole and turned it into platinum. In nine weeks. The government had been trying to do that with the Desire project for thirty years with no luck at all.

Bob came in about then. He was still white as a sheet, and his red hair was wet from what I expected had been a long, long bath. He'd caught some of Peetie's spatter, too.

—Go fool around on the street, I told him. —See what the talk is. Everybody knew Peetie. Maybe he had some friends.

Bob looked at me like my brain was puff pastry.

—Peetie? Friends? Shit, Rat . . . They'll be celebrating down on Decatur Street. That sonofabitch couldn't buy a piece of ass.

—Go talk, I said. —Even the friendless got rights.

—I keep hearing that. Bob nodded. —They say it all the time.

When he left, I sat back, gave my chair a turn, and stared out the window. Down below, the Broad Street viaduct was pulsing with traffic the way it did all day long. I knew whoever did the hit on Peetie was probably on his way back to Detroit or Toledo or wherever Burnucci's people had brought him from. We'd find a stolen car out off Interstate 10 or parked in a shopping mall somewhere. Maybe we'd find the rifle, a couple of shells. But that wasn't going to take us anywhere. The rifle would have been bought legitimately in Fresno and stolen in El Paso or some such thing.

I just kind of let my mind drift then. Sometimes I work that way. You let your thoughts go their own way. Maybe they know better than you do. Then it come to me that Amadeo's letting the judge set a trial date—when he knew he was gonna ask for a continuance—was just to flush Peetie out.

Goddammit, I should have reckoned on that, taken precautions. I could have shipped him by air to Shreveport or Biloxi. It didn't need to happen. A couple of hours before, we had Burnucci up against the wall. Now we had 420 pounds of fresh-killed dark meat coming in from Baton Rouge, and I reckoned Burnucci's heart condition was gonna improve real soon.

I been at this too long, I was thinking. It's a terrible job for people who don't give a damn. Anyhow, I'm losing my edge. Five years ago, they'd never been able to follow me to Baton Rouge. But that was five years ago.

See, I had this theory. Nobody ought to be a cop longer than ten years. That's the limit. You top out at five, and by the time you make ten, you're numb. If you're still on the street, you either don't care what goes down or you kick the shit out of everybody. If you're up the ranks, all you think about is how it'll play on TV and in the papers. Maybe I could teach in a criminology program or start that career in politics I'd been thinking about. Or go work for Housing Authority security. That's easy work. Nobody expects anything of you when you work in the projects. Fisher project is Dodge City, Iberville is Tombstone. Desire? How would you like to do a nice long tour in Beirut?

I was staring at the floor by then, doing the first draft of a resignation letter in my head. Then my eyes fell on that bright gold ticket in the trash can. Don't ask me why I reached down and picked it out of there. Maybe it was that the happiest thought I'd had all day was just to sit out the evening with Denise and Wes—even if it was at a damned rock concert that had to bring back a past I couldn't use—and didn't need.

The New Orleans DA's office looks like the city room at a big successful newspaper. Desks all out on this big floor, closed offices for the big shots along the outer walls where they get rugs and windows and paintings and such like.

Denise was still out in the bull pen. She'd be a couple of years moving into one of those offices where you could see outside. But she'd move, all right. See, her father had been Orleans Parish DA for years. There'd even been talk about his running for governor till things went wrong, then wronger, and Drew Lemoyne had ended up dead. People around town counted him a hero in the war against crime, and nobody pays me for saying any different. What Wes Colvin and Denise and I know stays right where it is.

She was sitting at her desk when I walked in, with Wes, back from the Desire project, lounging in a chair across from her. It was after hours, and the other desks were empty. When I told them I was thinking of throwing it over, they both looked shocked.

—In a pig's ass, Wes burst out.

—In an ox's tail, Denise chortled, still thinking about that lunch we'd bought her.

Wes got serious. —Who suspected Burnucci's folks were going to play Old Chicago on this thing?

—I get paid to suspect, I said.

—Forget it and come to the concert with us, Wes said. —Danny Bynum is all right.

—How'd the rally go? Denise asked him.

—My ears are cleaned and my sinuses blown. Jesus, those rockers use big speakers. But that Bynum kid knows what he's doing. He'd play 'em a number, then preach for five minutes. Putting down drugs, dealers. Telling them everyone knows who's dealing. Why not turn them in to the cops and save a few lives? Then he'd give 'em some more music. There must have been a couple of thousand kids there ... right out in the middle of one of those courts. They loved it.

It was nice the way they'd turned the conversation off Peetie and my fuck-up. It didn't make me feel any better, but it was a good loving try.

Wes stood up and looked at his watch. —You guys want to make the Dome now? Supper afterward?

When we got to the Superdome, it was, you could say, festive. Seemed like everybody in New Orleans under twenty was there. For some reason, they all had some kind of white bands wrapped around their heads. It looked like a samurai warriors' convention.

—What's that? I asked Wes, pointing at one of the kids.

—The headband? Danny Bynum wears one at all his concerts.

—Remember Michael Jackson's glove? Denise grinned.

—Who?

—Never mind.

We managed to push through the confusion and yelling and get inside the Dome lobby without me pulling my badge. Hell, even the ushers and ticket-takers had on those damned white headbands. I kept expecting to see some Japanese characters on them, the kind kamikaze pilots wore when they headed out for our ships. But the kids were peaceful enough. You might even call them well-behaved.

—How do we get to the box seats? I asked Denise. She gave me a blank look.

—Ours are in the press section, aren't they, Wes?

—Yeah...

—Wait a minute, I said, pulling out my ticket as we neared the passageway. —Didn't you send this over to my office?

Denise compared my ticket with the ones Wes was holding. —No, she said. —When you said you didn't want to go, I...understood.

—The tickets don't even look the same, Wes noted.

Before we could say much more, we were at the turnstile. When the ticket-taker saw mine, he gestured over to some guy who looked like a supervisor. They both studied the ticket like it was evidence. The supervisor looked at a clipboard he was carrying.

—Captain Trapp?

—Right.

—Come with me, please.

I shrugged and gave Denise and Wes a good-bye glance. —I'll see you afterward, I said.

—Maybe not, Denise trilled, giving me that romantic smile of hers. —Maybe...you'll be reliving the past.

—Shit, I said just before I was beyond earshot. —Who wants to go through anything twice?

—People in love, Denise yelled after me. —Who've found each other at last...

I could see Wes putting his hand over her mouth, then I was going through this dark corridor into some kind of booth or box. Sure enough, it was one of the season boxes they lease for Saints football games. It looked empty, the lights were low, the furnishings like I wished I had at my place. When the door closed behind me, I realized it wasn't quite empty. There was a chromium bar on the far side, and a bartender standing behind, wearing one of those headbands, looked like he was trying to be part of the decor.

—What can I serve you, sir?

—You got Irish whisky?

—Bushmills? Jameson?

—Black Bush. Triple. No rocks, no waves.

What he handed me was better than a triple. It was a water glass full. I found myself a seat near the front of the box and looked down and out through the plate glass into the auditorium. It was filling up fast, and the stage, still unlighted, shadowy, had all kinds of technicians or whatever they call them tinkering with the electronics.

Just then I noticed that there was an enormous TV screen built into the wall on my left. It was stuttering into life, and I could see the same people on it as I could see looking down. The sound came on, and I could hear somebody working a guitar and somebody else on keyboard. The visuals kind of got me, because the camera angle was different from mine, and I could see what I knew to be the same people doing the same things simultaneously, but not quite identical. A mighty strange way to see the world.

I sipped on my whisky and waited. It seemed like all of a sudden the techs on stage vanished, and the whole damned place went silent. I mean like no coughs, no shuffling. Billy Graham never had it so quiet. Then I could see that there were people on stage. It was too dark down there to make them out, but they were there. That's when I realized I was hearing a voice, that I'd been hearing it for a second or a minute—or a week. High, soft, like a sigh. It built and came up, and you could almost feel the way that audience below was turning toward it, seeking where it was coming from, leaning into it. But it was coming from everywhere, soft, asexual, anguished, tender, but present, dominating.

When the instruments came in over it at maximum volume, I almost dropped my glass. It was like all that electronic gear was dedicated to pushing that sob, that croon right out of existence. But it didn't. Like it couldn't. The voice kept building into and over that mass of micro-chipped sound like it didn't even know the machinery was there. Then a baby spot hit, and I got my first look at Danny Bynum.

He was as light as his mother, and even with the distance and the plate glass between us I could see that he had the same high cheekbones, the curly blue-black hair, the dark eyes that had stayed with me, despite what Wes had said, all the way back from Germany ten years ago.

> . . . Wise child, what a wise child,
> what a wise child you must be . . .
> You know who threw you into the world,
> who drew you out of the sea.
> Is it true, is it true, is it true what you say?
> You know who churned the Milky Way,
> who gave you night and gave you day?
> Pity me, can't you see that I'll never be free
> till I'm a wise child too?
> I've got to find his place, see his face,
> and say, Daddy I'm just like you . . .
> I wanna be a wise child too . . .
> I wanna be a wise child too . . .

It ended like it started, with that something like a sigh, something like a sob, only this time it fell beneath the music, merging, blurring, like the singer had gone on too long, gone out too far and now was losing himself in that starry reflective sea he had risen from sometime out of time ago.

When the last echo had slipped below hearing, the whole Superdome was dead still. Then the applause started welling up like waves on Danny Bynum's sea.

It's not my kind of music. The Germans got me into string quartets almost as soon as they had me eating *Kalbs-braten* and *Schnitzel*. But then you don't have to be into architecture to have your socks knocked off by the Taj Mahal. Camille's little boy was more than a rocker. He could tell a story in three minutes with the help of a handful of whackerboxes like nobody I'd heard in a long time. Maybe it was the old connection, maybe it was the whisky, but I made a note to go buy his album. I wanted to hear "Wise Child" again.

Before the next number started, before I could even consider just where all that sadness, all that wistfulness had come from, I heard or felt someone close by. I turned my head to tell the bartender I was doing just fine. But even in the shadows, the semi-darkness, I could see it wasn't the bartender sitting in a chair a few feet from me.

—Ralph...?

Her curly hair was still the color of burnished gunmetal, and she was wearing an off-white dress with a deep circular neckline. Her skin was the tone of light chamois, and her eyes were enormous and dark. Maybe in bright light she'd show the years, but not then. She was everything I remembered, everything I'd lost a long, long time ago.

—Hello, Camille, I almost whispered, stretching out

my hand to meet hers as she reached toward me, and the music began once more.

—I'm surprised, she said.

—Oh? I thought... You didn't send me a ticket?

Camille shook her head. —I wanted to call you. I almost did from the hotel this afternoon. Danny was out at the project, and I stared at the phone.

—But you didn't pick it up?

—No. I didn't think... I've got no business dropping back into your life as if...

—I don't know. You had your momma tell me we'd meet somewhere down the road.

Her eyes grew even larger. —You remember that?

—I remember you. Everything that had to do with you.

The bartender gave her an excuse to look away. He put something large and colorful down on an endtable, and Camille picked it up and ran her finger around the rim of the glass.

—Then... I guess this is... down the road.

—It better be, I said. —The road don't go on forever. So how's the weather in L.A.?

She threw back her head and laughed. —You can find that out on the TV. Is that all you want to ask?

I found I'd tossed back half my Black Bush since I realized who was in the box with me. No, that wasn't all I wanted to ask, but I was gonna be double goddamned if I'd ask her... Why? Much less, Who?

—You got something in mind? Your boy's famous, you're both rich, you live in Los Angeles, and we used to know each other a while back. You want me to ask how your husband's doing?

This time the laugh was bitter, resentful. —I don't have a husband, she said.

—What do you know? Did you walk off and forget where you left him?

She looked like I'd thrown my whisky in her face.

—I . . . never got married, she told me, her eyes on mine again. —What about your wife?

—Same as the weather in L.A. Nothing to talk about.

—I'm sorry.

—Nothing to be sorry about. I never had one. The women kept finding something better to do.

I bit my tongue. It wasn't me. Somebody else was using my voice. Camille smiled softly.

—I wish I had a dollar for every time I've thought about the last time we were together.

—You've got a lot more bucks than that. Where do you live? Beverly Hills?

—Brentwood. Almost down to the ocean.

—Must be the nicest housing project in the whole wide world, I said.

—Do you remember that last night?

—Sam Cotshaw's place. Across the court from your momma's. Sam was off at some kind of political meeting. You were wearing this blue-green dress . . .

Camille looked away again, one hand at her throat. In the soft light, I could see tears glistening in her eyes.

—It cost seventeen-fifty. It was the nicest dress I ever had. You gave it to me because . . .

—. . . because I didn't know you'd be wearing hundred-and-seventy-five-dollar dresses a day or so later.

—I wanted to tell you. I tried to tell you, but . . .

—Me telling you how much I loved you kept getting in the way.

I didn't want to do what I was doing. If we'd had it out that night twenty years ago, maybe I wouldn't have, but it felt like the next day to me, like that sonofabitch in his white Cadillac was sitting outside waiting, rich, faceless, sure of himself. Good thing for him it was all in my mind. Because now I carry a gun.

I was about to say something more, and Camille was looking like she wanted to be anywhere else in the world, when all of a sudden I found myself turning back toward the stage where Danny and Desire Project were still performing. Or should have been.

But just as I looked down, Danny faltered in the middle of a song, his guitar dropping to hang by its braided cord. He reached up and touched that white headband like it was too tight. His fingers caught in it, and it looked as if he was pulling a puppet's head—his own head—to one side as hard as he could. Then he did a little turn, fell into the microphone stand, and landed on the plank stage floor so heavily that we could hear it upstairs in the box.

For a fraction of a second, I wondered if it was one of those surprise endings or weird things rockers do nowadays. I glanced over at Camille, but her expression told me I was wrong. She was standing, staring down at the stage, her lips parted, and the sound welling up out of her throat was the same one I'd heard coming from Danny when he opened the show.

CHAPTER

4

We must have been five minutes getting downstairs and backstage. The whole place was crazy, and I had to use my shoulder because nobody gave a damn about my badge. The kids with the white headbands were squealing, crying in one another's arms. In a stairwell, three girls were kneeling, praying, moaning. Dome security people were wandering here and there, muttering into walkie-talkies as if they had something to say. Off-duty cops who augmented the private force for big events were standing around. I saw Maxine Hawkins with a couple of big street cops standing in front of a door. That was where we were headed. Maxine was very smart. She always managed to be where the action was going down, and she knew what to do.

I pulled Camille through the last of the crowd and stood her in front of the door.

—Max, this is Bynum's mother.

Maxine nodded, opened the door, and Camille went through, already calling her boy's name.

—What happened? I asked Max. She shrugged.

—Were you watching?

—Yeah. I was up in a box.

—Then you saw what we did. The kid grabbed his head and went down.

—No wounds?

—Not a thing. Terry and Arquette went out and got him, she said, motioning toward the uniformed cops. I looked at them.

—I was a corpsman, Arquette said. —It looks like cardiac arrest. I was gonna give him CPR but his manager said leave him be. He'd be all right.

—Follow me, I said as I went inside.

Danny Bynum was stretched out on a sofa, his eyes half open. Camille was trying to get to him, but some dip with shaggy hair down to his shoulders was holding her back.

—Come on, Camille. Danny's going to be okay. He just needs a minute or two...

Some other guy was using one of those snap packets of smelling salts on the boy. You could see it was doing nothing for him at all.

—Cliff, let go of me, Camille was almost screaming. —Let me...

—Look, he gritted,—I don't need hysteria. We've got to get him back on that stage. If we don't make half the concert, we lose the house. We don't need to...

I stepped over and took hold of the guy who was trying to rouse Danny. He decided he'd better follow his arm.

—What the fuck...

Then I reached over and got my hand around Cliff's neck. I got a way of turning heads. By the time I had his face where I wanted it, his eyes were bugging a little. That's all right. In my line of work I've found that bugged eyes mean close attention.

—You people sent for an ambulance? I asked quietly.

—No ambulance, the one Camille had called Cliff choked out.

—Max, I called.

She opened the door and looked in. —Captain?

—Get me an ambulance over here fastest—and get the goddamned way cleared for them to come in and us to go out.

—We keep one downstairs on these concerts.

—Start CPR, Arquette.

Camille was beside her boy then, trying to get some sign of consciousness out of him, wiping the makeup off his face. Arquette eased her aside and began helping the kid breathe. I forgot I still had hold of Cliff and his flunky until I heard Cliff choking. I dropped him on the floor.

—You're in trouble, he coughed after he'd gotten his breath.

—Yeah, I said. —I stay that way. Always in trouble, never in doubt.

I tossed the other one over on top of him just as Wes and Denise came through the door.

—Is it bad? Denise asked, paying no attention to my little display of temper.

—Who knows, I said. —That freak over there checking his ribs didn't even send for the medics.

Wes followed my eyes. —Looks like he could use a checkup himself.

—If he opens his goddamned mouth again, you can make book on it.

Two medics came in like a northeast wind, and I moved Camille from beside the couch. She didn't want it that way, but she knew I was right. One medic took over CPR from Arquette while the other gave Danny a quick look, then tried a flashlight on his pupils. I was looking down over his shoulder. It didn't look like there were any irises at all.

—Shit, the medic said. —What does he use?

I turned to Camille. —Honey, you want to tell the man how Danny gets up for these things?

Camille looked confused. —I don't know what you mean, she said. —He doesn't...

The medic looked pissed. —Okay, we do it the hard way. Let's get him over to Charity.

—Take him to Sacre Coeur, I said. Charity Emergency was good, but I knew Camille would want the best for her son.

They had him on a gurney and down the hall before anyone realized they were going. Camille tried to follow, but I held her back.

—Let 'em do what they do, I told her. Then I turned to Denise. —This is Camille Bynum, I said. —She could use some help right now.

Denise nodded. —Denise Lemoyne, Camille. Wes and I are old friends of Captain Trapp.

—Where are they taking Danny? she asked, her voice soft, disengaged.

—The best hospital. Hotel Sacre Coeur, Wes said. —Denise has her car outside. She'll take you there.

—Will you, baby? I asked. Denise smiled, took Camille by the arm, and went out the way the medics had gone. I stayed behind with Wes. I was going over the dressing room as we talked.

—You look like business, he said.

—My pleasure is business, I grunted. —I can't help it.

—Any reason to think bad thoughts?

—I don't know. That medic was thinking dope.

—Yeah, but...

—...but you spent the afternoon listening to the boy telling how bad that shit is, how they ought to nail dealers to the nearest tree.

—The kid sounded like he meant it. But then...

—Yeah, I said. —Everybody means everything. For fifteen minutes.

—Danny Bynum made it for over an hour.

—So he's got a long sincerity span.

There wasn't much in the room to show that anybody had spent time in it. But then a dressing room at the Superdome is not what you'd call a permanent address. There was a canvas suitcase in the corner, a couple of costumes on hangers in an alcove like a closet. An L.A. Lakers jacket was dropped over the back of a chair. On the makeup table there was powder, a couple of jars of cold cream and makeup, and a huddle of eyebrow pencils and such. No drugs.

Then I saw Danny Bynum's white headband lying on the floor near the sofa, leaned down and picked it up. It unfolded in my hand. There were words scrawled on it in something that looked like grease pencil. I looked and read and frowned.

Father be with me now and always

it said. What the hell was that supposed to mean?

I pushed the headband into my pocket, and Wes and I walked back outside into the mob that had fallen silent by then, simply staring the way the gurney had gone, staring at us, staring at one another as if they kept expecting someone to tell them what had happened to their troubadour, and where the music had gone.

The facilities are the newest, but Hotel Sacre Coeur is the oldest hospital in New Orleans. The nuns must have put up tents for the feverish and wounded while Bienville was storming around the swamps trying to find out just what it was he'd claimed for France, what he was going to call the Isle d'Orléans. The Sisters of the Sacred Heart are still at it after almost three hundred years. Sister Mary Cecilia, who honchos the place, likes to compare notes with me.

—I've seen some terrible things right here in your emergency room, I told her one time.

—That's strange, she answered me back. —All I've ever seen was Jesus. Suffering.

The crucifixes and holy pictures on the walls are old. But the equipment is right now. The kids who intern at Sacre Coeur fall somewhere in between. They come in from LSU and Tulane medical schools hard-nosed and mean, up for mayhem, ready for gunshot and stab and dope and car crash and all the other miseries we've built for ourselves since we whipped yellow fever and malaria. But the nuns do a number on them. After a few months they start seeing *people* with gunshot wounds, stab wounds, people doped out, torn up from wrong left turns and crossing against the light.

Wes and I went in through the emergency-room door and found Denise and Camille sitting outside a cubicle blocked off with green curtains.

—What have we got? I asked Denise.

—Not much. The doctor asked Camille the same thing the medic wanted to know.

Camille was sitting close to tears, her hand locked on Denise's arm as if she had nothing else to hold onto.

—I told them the truth, Ralph. Danny doesn't use anything. I know he doesn't. I've been with him every day, every step of the way.

I nodded and moved toward the cubicle. A nurse coming out started to give me instructions. I showed her my badge without even slowing down.

Inside they were working on the boy. They'd cut away his costume and cleaned him off. His skin was even paler, lighter than it had seemed onstage. They had him on oxygen and were doing whatever they do. I moved up behind the guy who was giving orders.

—Trapp. Homicide. What's the word?

—What do you say, Rat?

—Eddie? Shit, I thought for a minute you were a real doctor. What the hell are you doing here so late?

—Trying to keep this household word alive.

—What happened?

—Cardiac arrest. You tell these fucking kids and you tell 'em...

—That's it? A twenty-year-old with a heart attack?

—Not exactly. If you speedball heroin and cocaine, you pays two hundred an ounce and you takes lots of chances.

—Dope. You're sure?

—Lab says so.

—His momma says he doesn't do that shit.

—Then his momma is either stupid or lying.

—I know his momma.

—Then you can pick which one. I'm telling you this kid is full of it. They say he was singing when it hit him.

—That's right.

—Christ, I'm surprised he could walk on stage after he took that hit.

—You find tracks?

—Look, I'm trying to remind him he's supposed to keep breathing. Eddie Lombard stepped back and told his nurse,—Let's see if we can get him up to the ICU now.

—I'll wait. You want to check with me when you're done? I'll be around.

—You got it. But what I know now is all I'm gonna know then. This kid pumps.

I moved out of the cubicle then, my mind freewheeling, working on its own. Either Danny Bynum was one more cheapshit hype type, or something funny was going down. We'd see, wouldn't we?

I found Camille in the hospital cafeteria. Denise and Wes were urging some good black coffee and chicory on her.

—Danny's still unconscious. They're moving him into ICU.

Camille sort of slumped like the bad news pierced her to the heart. —Anything else? she asked.

—The doctor says Danny was doing dope. I know the man. If he says it . . .

Camille's head snapped up. —I don't care what the man says. Danny never took drugs. Not ever.

I shrugged and glanced over at Wes and Denise.

—Camille, I tell you the tale I've been told. Your boy's had a heart attack. Brought on by a heroin-and-cocaine overdose.

She rose quickly, overturning her cup. Denise set it straight in the saucer.

—I'm going to be with my boy, Camille said, her voice cold and angry. —You know, that dope fiend they've got in intensive care upstairs.

I watched her go, feeling even more than I had earlier that it was time for me to give it over, find myself a new line of work.

—Nobody wants to hear what I told her, I said.

—She sounds like she knows what she's saying, Denise put in, her voice quiet but firm.

—Right. She knows, and Eddie Lombard is full of shit.

—No, Denise went on. —It's just that . . .

—If it's true, it's true, Wes said, but I could tell he was a holdout, too.

—Okay, folks, youall got another story?

—Out at the project today, Wes started, as if he'd just as soon not be saying anything.

—I'm listening.

—Danny got himself an argument going . . . after the talk and the concert.

—Huh?

—You know Tyrone Jefferson?

—Sure. Lost his pharmacy license for dealing. Ought to be doing consecutive tens except he was close to one of our local black legislators. Supposed to be Burnucci's head man in the project.

—Jefferson was there. Came on real strong with Danny when the band was packing up. Told the kid to haul ass, to stay out in L.A. and preach to his own. Said nobody needs him in New Orleans, especially in the projects. Who was Danny to be preaching when his mother used to peddle her ass.

—Tyrone said that?

—A bunch of Danny's people held him back. He wanted a piece of your old family druggist.

—Good for the kid.

—Yeah, Wes said. —That's how I felt. Still...

—Still what?

—Afterward, I rode back to the Royal Orleans in the kid's limo.

—All right.

—Danny's illegitimate.

—Well, shit, I believe I'm gonna faint.

Wes laughed out loud.

—It seemed to matter to him a lot? Denise asked.

—What?

—About... who his father is.

—At the hotel, Wes told her,—Danny and I had a drink. He said this date in New Orleans was a big thing for him.

—That's the way that prick Cliff, his manager, seemed to see it.

—No, not the concert. He said while he was here he was going to see his father for the first time.

I thought about that. Why not? Surely by now Camille had told the kid about that big white Cadillac.

—I guess that's what he was singing about, I said.
—But I'm not sure it's the best idea he ever had.

Denise looked like I'd said something wrong. —Why not?
she asked. —A boy should know his father. Shouldn't he?

—Depends, I said. —Maybe not.

—You know who his father is?

—No. I never had a name. If I had, his father would likely
be dead. All I ever heard was a white Cadillac car with a
couple of soldiers to make sure the niggers kept their distance while the Man picked up his new stuff.

—Rat . . . , Denise said. She made it sound more like an
insult than a nickname.

—Look, I went off with Uncle Sam about then, I told her.
—I don't know who his daddy is. All I said was, maybe he'd
do just as well letting it go on by.

Denise looked somber. —Unless he comes out of this,
maybe he'll never know.

I finished my coffee. —Better he live and know than die
and don't, I said after a moment.

—I'm glad you said that, Denise told me as she got up
from the table to go sit with Camille. —I really am.

—Me, too, I called after her as she headed for the elevator, and Wes gave me something like a knowing smile.

When I checked in with Eddie Lombard, he looked like he'd
been through a carwash tied to the top of a truck.

—Man, all I need is half a dozen drinks and home in the
sack, he told me.

—How about a really fine piece of butt? I asked him.

—Tomorrow. Ask her if she'll still want me tomorrow.

—I'm not sure she'd want you tonight, old son, I said.
—What do you know about the Bynum kid you didn't know
an hour ago?

—Strange, Eddie said. —Real strange. The kid doesn't
have any symptoms of a heavy user. He didn't sniff, and

he didn't shoot. I went over him with a glass, and there's not a sign on his body.

—So?

—So maybe the street's found a new way to pump. Rat, the kid's blood is full of cocaine and heroin. What do you want me to tell you?

—How you get full of it with no entry points?

—Up yours. That's cop's work. You tell me.

—You dumb asshole, if I had a degree in pathology . . .

—Okay, it's medical work. Let me see what I can do.

—Sweet. And, Eddie . . .

—Uh . . . ?

—She says she can make it in the morning. How about five A.M.?

—Jesus, you're an animal.

—Ain't we all?

I went back to my office in Central Lockup and found Maxine had checked in. We talked about her little job on Superdome security.

—Nothing to it, she said. —Lots of nice kids wanting to see Danny Bynum up close, touch him. You know . . .

—No, I don't, but I'll take your word. Anybody visit him before the show?

—What do you mean? The damned place was like Bourbon Street on a holiday weekend.

—You know Tyrone Jefferson?

—Little Ty? Sure. Who doesn't? If you swear you won't tell, I'll blow his lights out.

—You know his people?

—One or two. If you're asking, nobody showed at the concert who deals. Maybe you ought to check out the band. You can haul a real stash in a bass drum.

—You see they got back to their hotel?

Max nodded. —They're in the Royal Orleans. I doubt

they'll be doing the town tonight. They looked like somebody might have bent, folded, and stapled their meal ticket.

—His momma swears her boy was clean. Maybe his friends will say different.

—You want me to come along and introduce you?

—Sure.

We drove down Broad, across Canal, and took a right on Orleans to the Quarter. It was past peak hours, and only the folks who just can't get enough were still wandering around, looking in the windows of antiques stores, buying T-shirts, or drifting from bar to bar. Some people like Bourbon Street. I can do without it. The front is neon and jazz and lots of good food and laughs. Out back, it's mean and don't give an inch.

You can make a lot of money in the Quarter. Junk dealers buy beds and tables and nightstands in Europe, call 'em antiques, mark up the price a thousand percent, and move 'em on out to people from Dallas or Portland or Kansas City. The beer is two-fifty a whack, and mixed drinks run up to seven-fifty. When there's a Superbowl or the Sugar Bowl, the hotels jack up their room rates thirty or forty percent, and restaurants issue new menus.

But the money and the free style bring in everything. All the closet cases in the rural towns of the Deep South creep into New Orleans to do what they like to do. A lot of them never leave. Some of 'em settle in the Quarter. Some of 'em settle in St. Louis Cemetery No. 2, or out at Forest Lawn. Some of 'em go to the municipal burial plot because they thought it was a good idea not to carry ID. Did you ever see a man with perfectly groomed hair and fingernails, a Rolex Oyster, wearing a six-hundred-dollar suit, getting dropped into a grave in potter's field? Happens a lot. He goes down in his suit. The Rolex hangs around the property room for a while.

When a big event is in town, whores pour in from New

York and San Francisco. Their pimps get in fights with the local fauna. Sometimes tourists get caught in the cross fire. Couple of years ago, a guy from Canada got holed when a pair of street apes in fur coats and shades took to shooting at each other in front of the Monteleone Hotel. For myself, I don't mind. It keeps my blood going and my eyes wide open—if not bugged. But women and children and old folks always catch the strays. I don't like that.

The place is crawling with dealers. Half the business in the Quarter is dopers selling to one another. Lots of little mom-and-pop operations keep turning up dead two at a time in the trunk of a car or the tub of a ratty apartment because of those pressures of consolidation I was talking about.

The Royal Orleans is a fine hotel. It looks good, the location is good, the service is okay. Even the food is better than what you expect at a hotel.

Desire Project hadn't made it up to bed. They were sitting in the bar area next to the Rib Room with Arquette. Maxine had told him to carry them home and tuck them in. Arquette was drinking on duty and couldn't figure out whether he was protecting the band or keeping it under surveillance. When Max and I came up, he tried to hide his drink under his uniform cap.

—The way you do that is drink shots and keep a side of water on the table, I told him. —You can drop a shot-glass in your pocket. Or even into the water.

The boys nudged each other and laughed. Arquette faded off toward the men's room. I think he had to tidy up his pants.

Desire Project was four nice-looking kids, two white, two black. They didn't look sullen or mean, and they showed taste enough to keep giving Max long, loving looks.

She introduced me around. —Bobby Maxey, this is Captain Rat Trapp.

Bobby was a good-looking blond surfer with a smile and a kind of lost look in his eyes that said he really hoped you'd like him but he didn't give it much of a shot. Nobody would ever have to ask him where he was from. We shook hands and I looked past him to the next one.

—Zip Nelson.

Slender, black, clipped hair, heavy lids that worked for him. He could show you his eyes centimenter by centimeter, each gradation giving his whole face a different expression. I was getting the benign, mildly interested focus. He didn't offer to shake, and I didn't leave my hand in the air. He looked like East L.A. or a certain neighborhood in Long Beach. Scourge of the greasers, but brittle. I could give him hysterics without getting out of my chair, and he knew it.

—Rob Horner.

This one was out of a Scorsese movie. Pale, hard cold eyes that belonged on a creator or a killer. He didn't give a shit for anybody above or below the ground. Back in the old days when rock could still interest a grown-up, Jim Morrison had that look some nights. Maybe even Mick Jagger when he was pleading the devil's case.

—Lead guitar? I asked him.

—Yeah, he said, almost surprised. —You watch the band?

—No. I'm watching you.

The drummer was Pete Frye. A tall slender black kid, very dark, who ought to have been in college with a scholarship. Basketball or baseball, I couldn't figure which. But one day or night, somewhere or nowhere at all, he'd heard a sound, a certain rhythm, and now he was doing to drums what he might have done to a baseball or a backboard in school. On the other hand, by the time he was done with Desire Project, he could buy himself a college. That is, if there was any Desire Project left.

All in all, not too bad. I wasn't thinking of adopting any of 'em, but I'd seen worse. I saw worse every day. Horner was the one who interested me. I wondered if he liked Danny Bynum, but I didn't ask. I just asked them all about dope.

—We do a lot of beer, Bobby said in utter seriousness.

—Nobody does it, Pete told me. —Oh, hell, I smoke some grass on an afternoon sometimes, but that's it. The others nodded.

—Whisky was good enough for my old man, Rob Horner said deadpan. —It killed his ass.

—You from Jersey?

—Fairlawn.

—Nice town to be from.

He laughed. —As long as I can stay from it. The best thing in Jersey is the road to L.A.

—So Danny didn't do shit?

—No, Zip said. —If he had, we'd have known. And Ma Bell would have.

—Who's Ma Bell?

They looked at one another nervously. Bobby finally smiled at me. —That's Mrs. Bynum, Danny's mother. She makes the trips with us. If we try anything weird...

—She reaches out and touches us, Zip cackled. —I gave her the name.

—How does she like it? I asked.

—Fine. She knows we love her. When she heard us calling her that at rehearsal one night, she just leaned in the door and...

—...she said, The more I hear, the better you sound. Rob roared.

I liked the kids. Even Horner. They had a good thing,

and they knew it. No hidden currents so far as I could see. A Cub Scout troop with a terrific den mother, making twenty thousand a night. Bobby looked at me and cleared his throat.

—How's Danny, Captain Trapp? Is he gonna make it?

—I don't know, I said. —Maybe in the morning. You guys want to go by the hospital tomorrow, I'll send somebody around.

—Yeah, Maxine put in. —I had to use hotel security to get the TV and press out of here when we first brought them from the Dome.

—I wondered about that. It's kind of quiet.

—They're hanging around the hospital, she said with contempt. —Like buzzards.

Nobody likes the media unless you need to use them, I was thinking. Scavengers. But when nobody else will listen, you can always talk to a buzzard. One of my best friends is a big news bird. But with Wes and me, it's different. He never squats on my shoulder, and I don't feed him garbage.

—What happens if Danny goes down? I asked them. They looked like I shouldn't have asked.

—We're history, Horner rasped. —Like Full Tilt Boogie Band without Joplin.

Pete nodded. —We're good. Hell, everybody working is good one way or another. But Danny . . . he was our edge.

—Yeah, I said. —It comes right up out of the ground with him.

We made small talk for a few minutes more, then I sent them up to bed, planted Arquette outside their door.

—I don't know, I told Maxine.

—Look, she said. —What do you want them to tell you? Why put themselves on the line? If nothing had happened, they'd all be having a snort before bedtime. All this clean and upright doesn't bend the lab report.

—Madame, you're right. It's been a long day. You want a lift home?

I wanted her to say yes. I was tired, but not that tired. She just smiled and shook her head.

—See you in the morning, was all she said.

CHAPTER
5

I woke up in my place at the Olympia Apartments on St. Charles Avenue. It was just past six in the morning. I'm like a machine. Whatever goes down the night before, the eyes pop open at six. Ten years in the army did that. I got up and shaved and climbed into this nappy-looking sweatshirt and baggy pants I use for my morning do.

Outside, it was cool and humid. It was closer to autumn than to summer now and, by the time I started trotting, the air felt like champagne in my lungs. I took a left running into Audubon Park and felt like I could circumnavigate the place three times before breakfast. Not quite. The knees are unpredictable. The wind comes and goes. These muscles in the front of my legs begin to feel like I was being nailed to a passing tree.

But you can put your mind on the oak trees with limbs thicker than a man, which almost touch the ground from their weight and years. You can hear the dry magnolia leaves crackling underfoot, the birds just waking, wondering who the hell is threshing around down in the basement of their world. You can lose yourself along the lagoon and watch bass rise and snap a dragonfly out of the air when it dips for a quick dangerous drink.

Then, when you've run off all your spunk, the years come up and pop you in the gut, you can slow down and start walking just as the town begins to wake up. The cars come coughing out of their garages, the people, bleary-eyed, get themselves together to go do another day's work.

Coming back from the park, I was trying to sort things out. I don't like contradictions. I never did. I found out early on that contradictions mean you haven't got all the pieces, or you haven't thought the problem through.

Things are mostly the way they seem. I mean, you take a situation and put it together piece by piece. When everything fits, you back away and see the whole. And that's the way it is.

This thing with Danny Bynum wasn't working. That meant pieces were missing or I didn't have my brain in gear. Maybe both. I could dig that the kid was doping and Camille didn't know. You want to bet your uphol-stered middle-class ass that your kid don't toke? But like the grave-robbers down in pathology say, there's always an ingestion point. Gimme a few little bruises in the crook of his arm, some dissolved mucus membrane, and all I can tell Camille is, Sorry, baby.

But I got to have that ingestion point. That day I was going to get it. If I had to fly in some high-priced pa-thologist from Houston or L.A. to do it. That is, if I didn't start getting heat from my opposite number in Narcotics or from the boys upstairs who don't spend a lot of their time admiring my style.

You'd think all my miseries would be from the old-timers who couldn't quite buy a black captain of police. Old white segs who carry their attitudes right up the ladder and over into retirement, right? Wrong. It was the black top cops who leaned on me. They liked the way I dressed. They liked the case-clearance ratio I gave them. But they didn't like my ways. Said I policed like the whites used to do it in the old days. God forbid I should lay hands on a suspect with anything but control and custody in mind. One of the old white guys I partnered with for a while thought I was the best thing he'd seen since sliced bread.

—You get your style from the army, son?

—Yep. I got to where they liked me to interrogate East German suspects. Blacks scared the shit out of 'em.

He laughed at that, but his face was serious. —Breaking heads has got to be done just right. If you do it for a laugh, they ought to throw you in the bull pen with the scum. You only do it to get what you need.

—Yeah, I said, remembering what I'd done a couple of times to get what I needed. —That's civilization.

Sergeant Murray was right, though. If I got solid reason to believe you know what I need to know, I'll pulverize your kidneys to get it. If not, you don't even exist. This is a business, not a sport. But my superiors don't want to do business. They want community relations. They want folks to be nice—so they can enjoy being big shots with no problems.

But that shit fades when you step outside Brennan's Restaurant or your uptown neighborhood boutique. The streets are worse than they ever were, and they ought to hand rookies a big-game license when they come out of the academy. How do you community relate with some clown who rapes girls, then shoots 'em in the back of the head while they're putting their clothes back on? You want the killer, or you want me to waltz with every two-bit mother-hurting punk I pick up? I won't dance, don't ask me.

I needed something, but I couldn't figure where I was going to get it. I didn't even know for sure what it was.

My first shot was Eddie Lombard. He'd be nearing the end of his shift in emergency about now, and maybe he'd know something he hadn't last night.

Eddie keeps a cot down in the basement of Sacre Coeur. It's dark and quiet and damp, and nobody comes down just to shoot the shit.

He was taking a nap. He does that before he goes home to bed. He's got three kids under five years old, and a wife who doesn't understand. I wish somebody would introduce me to a wife who does understand. There's gotta be one somewhere. Or maybe she ran out on her man the same day she come to understand. Eddie snapped awake when he heard me pouring his coffee.

—Easy, I told him. —The Bomb just dropped and the casualties are on the way in. Have a cup first.

He laughed and drank. CDM, the best coffee on the planet. Eddie likes to say it reminds him of me: black, strong, rich.

After a couple of gulps, he reached in a pocket of his whites and pulled out a dirty crumpled piece of paper.

—Your boy Danny's situation has shifted from odd to weird.

—Say on, my man.

—I ordered another blood test. Looking for something out of the ordinary. There it was. Big as whale turds and twice as peculiar. DMSO.

—Your momma.

—Dimethyl sulfoxide.

—Shit, man . . .

—It's a solvent. You can dissolve stuff in it. Like coke and heroin.

—All right. You can use ether, too.

—No, no . . . I'm not talking free-basing. This stuff will

carry a compound right through the skin . . . into the bloodstream. In seconds.

That stopped me. Eddie and I stared at each other for a while.

—So you dissolve your dope in this DSOM . . .

—DMSO, yeah. And you rub it on your skin . . .

—. . . and you've got yourself a package.

Eddie nodded. —We used a gas chromatograph. DMSO's like carbon tet. It hangs around.

—So we got a kid who found a new way to pump.

Eddie nodded. —They use a lot of DMSO out in Nevada and California. It's great for carrying arthritis drugs to a site. Sooner or later somebody had to drop some hash or horse or coke into it. Now does that convince you the kid's a doper?

—Yeah. Maybe it'll convince his momma, too. You know how Danny's coming along?

Eddie shrugged. —This is just us talking?

—You need it that way?

—Right. After we talk, it's off the record and out of your mind.

—You got it.

—I'm not a neurologist, but I think what you got is a grocery bag full of blood and guts up there, he said. —The first EEG was barely spiking. My bet is, he's gone.

I left Eddie and went upstairs. Maybe they'd told Camille, maybe not. Either way, I thought it might be nice if I dropped by. Eddie could be wrong. Danny might pull through on the far side of this thing. Twenty used to be a magic age. You could do anything, if they'd just tell you how. But I wouldn't bet my Mississippi plantation on Eddie Lombard being wrong, and most of the magic has gone.

They'd moved Danny into an intensive care suite. On

the fourth floor, of course. Local folks who could paper their walls with hundred-dollar bills and Latin American types who could buy the walls didn't like their people lying in an ICU with the common trash. So Sacre Coeur had a floor of suites set aside to help pay the rent for the rest of us. At $3,500 a day, you could subsidize quite a few old folks and poor people—and keep your loved one free of contamination.

I got off the elevator and started down the corridor. None of the rush and bustle and pushcarts left around up there. No, this was the Claridges of hospital halls. Rug on the floor, a love seat and chairs here and there, mirrors and pictures on the walls. Just your basic sick-rich hangout.

As I came up on the suite where Danny Bynum was supposed to be, I saw this big ugly white guy. He was standing in front of a door down the hall looking me over. Not like he was just curious what a shade was doing in the high-rent district. Not even like he was afraid the neighborhood might be going to hell. More like he was wondering if he ought to step up and work on my face.

I motioned the guy over, but he just ignored me.

—You, I said. —Come here. Keep your hands where I can see 'em.

He came, all right. Pulling a Beretta .38 out of a holster under his arm like he was trying to figure whether to crack me upside my head or shoot me in the nose. I let him get closer than I should have because I like to work that way. Then I kicked him in the cods and slapped the automatic down the hall. A nun rounded the corner, and the gun skittered up against her foot. I had my man shoved up into the door where he'd been standing by then. His arm was behind his back and over his head. He was starting to breathe hard and moan as the nun walked up to us looking as if she didn't believe what she was seeing.

—This is a . . . hospital.

—Good, Sister. I'm glad to know that, because this guy's gonna . . .

—You can't . . .

—Yes, Sister, I can. I really can. Captain Ralph Trapp, NOPD. This man drew a weapon when I approached him.

—Oh . . .

—You sonofabitch, my man was muttering. I cranked him up another three inches. He went to his toes like Baryshnikov. Another inch or so and he'd do his human fly imitation on the door.

—Not in front of the nun, scumbag. Sister, you'll excuse us, won't you?

She backed away, still staring. Then she felt her foot hit the pistol, leaned down, picked it up, and brought it over to me.

—Do you have some identification? she asked me.

—Ah, yes. I do. But as you can see . . . tell you what. Mention my name downstairs to Sister Mary Cecilia. Tell her there's a big black guy up on four beating up a big white guy with a gun. Then tell her my name.

She looked a little doubtful, but there wasn't much else she could do. While she and I had been talking, the hard man I had hold of was trying to scratch a hole in the door to crawl through—or else he was scratching out a message. I think it must have been that last, because the door opened and there was another one who looked just like him. I mean the way bookends look alike. I figured he'd probably have himself a Beretta, too—one serial number higher or lower—so I shoved my sucker into him and watched them wrestle on the floor for a moment or two.

While I was pulling the clip from Bookend Number One's gun and levering out the slug in the chamber, I looked across the sitting room. It was in shadow, with the blinds drawn to keep out the morning sun, but I could see through to the next room where the patient must be. After maybe ten seconds, there stood Nick Burnucci, Mr. X's son. With an Uzi submachine gun cradled in his arm like he was expecting St. Valentine to drop by.

—What do you say, Nick? I called out as his twins unraveled themselves.

—Who the fuck are you? You want to be a paying customer in this place?

—Ralph Trapp. NOPD. You want to tell your men to show me their licenses? Maybe I better check that piece of yours, too. Just to see if it's semi or full auto.

Nick hesitated, then decided to play it cool. He couldn't afford another mistake. He'd used up his credit with his old man already. His carelessness checking out his help at the Vegas East had been responsible for Mr. X's indictment. Another mistake like that and his cousin Kenny would be the next *capo*.

Nick gestured at the Bookends. As they fumbled out their wallets, he protested.

—My father is very sick. Why you hassling us? You looking to get on the pad?

Nick Burnucci was probably a good-looking man twenty years ago. I bet he was tall and slim with dark hair and eyes, long lashes, kind of dramatic firm jawline that might make you think he was gonna look like a *capo da tutti capi* when he was forty. It hadn't worked that way. Even in the shadowed room you could see the flab in his face, the extra flesh gathered around his belt. He looked like he hadn't gotten a good night's sleep in that twenty years. He was never gonna look like a *capo* even if Mr. X handed him the town in an empty cement sack.

And he'd never hold on to it, either. Across the room, I could see the fear in his eyes. Not just of me, of this big scary nigger who filled the door and played soldiers with his soldiers. Of everything. Of how it felt to make a living the way he did with every corner and doorway and shadow as likely as the last—or the next—to hold that mechanic or cowboy your enemies have sent to expel you from the fraternity.

—Keep your hoods out of the hallway, Burnucci. Set a perimeter in here. You hear me?

—This is gonna cost you, spook.

I felt my jaw tighten. Old man Burnucci had a reputation as a racist. With him, it wasn't how you dressed. It wasn't class or education. Word was, he hated the color of some men's skins, and the color he hated most was basic black. I hadn't heard it of Nick, but blood tells.

—Last guy called me that had surgery. To get my foot out of his ass, I told him. —If you want a gun in the hall, call the superintendent of police and tell him your story. I'm gonna be visiting around here a lot. If I find one of these ding-dongs out there, I'm gonna ice him down. The same way Peetie Postum got iced. *Capice?*

Nick heard, and found a new way to look haggard. The boys on the floor heard. I think they believed. I tossed the Beretta at one of them. He wasn't looking, and it caught him in the side of the head. Maybe it was the right one. I didn't give a shit. Always end your sentences with a period.

I walked back down the hall and knocked on the door of Danny Bynum's suite. A nurse came to the door. I guess she must have been very competent. She looked like a trucker from Lake Charles coming back from a serious drunk. Camille came in from the other room and managed a smile for me. I gave her a quick hug as my eyes followed the nurse back into the room where Danny was lying.

It looked like a cross between a high-tech lab and the situation room we had in West Berlin. Machines on top of machines. Digital read-outs, runny little lines like a Pong game, wires and tubes and all the rest of it running toward a bed I couldn't quite see, to monitor what was left of the life of a kid I had never even met. I felt a great sadness and turned my gaze away.

—He's sleeping, Camille told me, her eyes as full of terror as Nick Burnucci's. —In a few days, he's going to wake up and . . .

—What have they told you, Camille?

—If I believed everything they've said . . . He's still alive, Ralph. I've gotten the best specialist around. He's going to give Danny back to me.

Was I supposed to argue with her? I knew what Eddie Lombard had told me, but he wasn't going to be the doctor on the case, and I wasn't going to quote him. Camille had probably bought herself a doctor as expensive as this suite, and he'd take his time and run the meter before he told her whatever the truth might be. Partly to make the bucks big-time doctors make. Partly to be sure.

—Danny looks so healthy now. I think he's getting better, and . . .

—Camille . . .

—. . . maybe tomorrow . . .

—Camille.

She stopped talking when I barked at her. Her lips quivered and I could see tears gathering in her eyes. I remembered my mother saying, You don't let go a child easy. But you do let go. She'd been talking about me going into the army. I guess the same thing holds with letting go altogether.

—Don't say what you're going to say, Ralph. Please . . . you don't understand. If you knew . . .

I decided to keep my mouth shut. After a day or two, she'd have a raft of people around her who get paid to tell folks terrible things. I wondered whether I should talk to her about what Eddie Lombard had discovered. What the hell.

—Camille, we've got proof now that Danny overdosed.

—No, damn it. I told you, I told everyone...

—Stop telling, because you're wrong. That's what caused the cardiac arrest. He used DMSO to give it to himself.

She had been about to shout me down, but her voice caught in her throat. She looked puzzled, as if she couldn't quite understand.

—What?

—It's a solvent. A way of shooting up without using a needle. They found DMSO with the drugs in his blood.

—If they did, then somebody put it there. Not Danny.

—Damn it to hell, Camille, that'd mean somebody wanted Danny dead. What'd be their motive? Haven't you picked up no smarts in twenty years?

That stung her and shut her up. But I knew the answer to my own question. No, she hadn't. She'd been looking for the ticket out of Desire the last time I saw her, and she'd gotten it from somebody who punched her, not the ticket. She hadn't even noticed that the back of the ticket named a price: you pay and you pay and you pay.

Just then there was a knock, and Denise came through the door. She and Camille exchanged hugs. Then she came over to me while Camille went in to check on Danny. I filled her in on what I knew.

—Rat, could Camille be right? Are you going to treat it as a case?

—Get off, Denise. I've got a case—Peetie's. I think I'm gonna go out and splash around in the dirty water and see what makes for the rocks.

She shook her head and smiled. —God, the way you do business.

—Sweet woman, nothing communicates like a big mean

bull cop with his head down, breaking through the un-
derbrush.

—Be careful or the Justice Department will assign a man
just to watch you. You're a walking civil rights violation.

—Those fed bastards got all they can do to keep their
own pad clean. Anyhow, I knew a long time ago this civil
rights thing was going too far. Once in Berlin the Reds
had two of our Germans, getting ready to carry 'em back
East. My people wouldn't let me use an icepick on this
Czech bastard we scooped up.

—So you lost your Germans?

—Oh, no. When the boss left, I stripped a light cord,
plugged in one end, and dropped the other in a full bath-
tub. Then I pushed the sonofabitch's arm in it and told
him his head was next. Direct current. Better than a tele-
gram.

Denise is so fine, so Uptown, so New South. I love the
woman and she loves me, but my Germans would be
doing time in the Lubyanka if she'd been there. She shook
her head as if to say, This is just not the world I counted
on. Right. I didn't do the blueprint, either. But I sure as
hell can read it.

—Maybe you can talk Camille into going out for lunch.
I got to get to work, I told Denise.

—Behave yourself.

—Behave is a big wide word, dolly.

You drive down off the Interstate 10 at Louisa Street, you
make a few turns and find yourself in one of the biggest
public housing projects in the world. Desire project. Almost twenty thousand people living in a few square blocks.

Once, a long time ago, somebody had the idea you
could build cheap public housing for people who just
weren't gonna make it up to State Street or Audubon
Place in this lifetime. It wasn't gonna be fancy, but it

would be nice and clean, room for flowers out front, space for the kids to play. Little two- and three-bedroom apartments, dignity, security, all that bullshit.

The people who had the idea never lived there, of course. They never meant to. They were doing something for other folks. God help me if somebody goes to do something kind and good for me. It'll end up like Desire more times than not.

Forty years after the dreams, it's hell on a vacant lot. You know it going in. From a little distance, the place looks all right, but you start seeing how there's no grass in the open spaces, only garbage and trash and maybe a dead dog hit by a car or set fire to by the punks. How there's old tires and even stripped cars parked along the curbs. You see where creeps have used spray paint to put graffiti on the tan bricks, and broke-out windows everywhere. You go into a hallway and see sheetrock ripped out and smell piss in the stairwells.

You see kids and old folks sitting on the stoops with nowhere to go and nothing to do, nothing to be but stoop-sitters. You watch the bloods go by giving you hard eyes, carrying a sharpened comb in their back pocket or a bicycle chain looped around their wrist. Young girls pass, and you read their eyes and know by the time they're twelve they've been had every way they can be had, and that they've got nothing left to sell, nothing to give away but their cute little asses.

There aren't many grown men around that you can see because the welfare rules cut aid if there's an able-bodied man living in an apartment. They come at night to get what they want, and the women just keep pumping more kids into the System. If you have yourself half a dozen bastards got on you by God knows who, and who cares, you can make out pretty good on ADC. Every now and again the government goes through and flushes off some of the loafers or offers job training or some such. It comes to nothing, because leaving Desire for work always means coming back to Desire at night. You take Desire with you wherever you go.

Hopelessness, buried frenzy, craziness hangs in the air at Desire. One day they're gonna have to take the people out, make them leave everything they have there, and promise not to look back. Then burn the place to the ground. Like you burn the clothes and goods of plague victims.

I should know. I was born and raised in Desire. My mother died there while I was in the service. On mother's day—not the holiday the florists made up, but the day welfare and Social Security and ADC checks turn up in the mailbox at Desire—my mother started out to cash her little check at the dry cleaners where her cousin worked. One of the shitbags hanging around decided he needed it for heroin. Momma fought him, and he cut her up. She bled to death on her front stoop before they could find an ambulance driver who'd come into the project. They caught the punk about an hour later at a grocery saying he was her son, trying to cash her check. They gave him ten years because he was young and a first offender. He picked up a lot of good time in prison and got out after two years.

They found him face down in a pile of dogshit over on Abundance Street about six weeks after I got home. Somebody had broken his neck.

Another thing about Desire: it's a doper's paradise. Kind of like a discount warehouse. If they don't have it in stock, they can turn it for you in twenty minutes. The kids, the little boys and girls, are the runners. The teenage boys sell and collect. Some of the stuff is put together right there on the premises. All the people say Tyrone Jefferson is the resident capitalist, but Tyrone is never on the scene when the feds come in like a herd of elephants and make a little bust that everybody knew was coming a week before. NOPD's narcs nicked him once, but that was a long time ago.

I knew Tyrone. We went to school together. He was a shitass in the third grade, and he'd had lots of time to refine and polish. He was an interstate asshole by then, trying for continental status. Tyrone was smart all right. He went to college and got him a pharmacist's ticket, but they busted him for dealing out of his brother's drugstore before he'd had it two years. They put him away for a couple to think it over. He did. He decided to be smarter. One of the narcs likes to say Tyrone would sell you his mother for a dollar and hand you back eighty-five cents. Except she died pulled way out on speed four or five years ago. Five will get you fifty Tyrone charged her for the dose that killed her.

I got nothing personal against Tyrone. But word had it he was Burnucci's man. This looked like a good time and place to go splashing. If I could hang anything on Tyrone, he might tell me what I wanted to know. But I had to be careful how I approached him. You never know when a junkie will go crazy and cut you in two. And nobody hung out with Tyrone except junkies.

I parked outside the manager's office because they won't usually pull the tires off a strange car if they know the office help is watching. Even in Desire, sometimes people will get pissed off and tell all. Not often enough to make book, but sometimes.

The lady at the counter looked up when I walked in. Then she did this number with her eyes. I believe she hadn't seen a well-dressed black stranger in those parts for some time.

—Yes? Can I help you?
—Lady, I know you can.

—I'll certainly try. You're not here for a rental?

—Uh, no. Not at present.

—Ummmm.

—I'm looking for an old friend, schoolmate of mine from years back.

—We have a register, but it's really not complete at all. You see...

—Tyrone Jefferson's the name.

This woman had been going over me with her eyes like a furrier does a pelt. All of a sudden, winter come. I could have used a few pelts myself.

—That's... your friend?

—Uh...

—I thought you looked too good to be true. Are you a pimp or a dealer? You don't look like a punk.

—I... you see...

—I hope the cops come down on both of you.

—Honey, honey, turn it on back down. Damn it, I *am* the cops.

—You what?

I finally got straight with the lady. Seems Tyrone was making enemies he didn't need all over the project. Some people, my lady at the desk included, were starting to get the idea that Desire didn't *have* to be hell. It didn't say so in the housing regs. She gave me detailed directions, including where old Tyrone liked to keep his pickets.

Yes, I said pickets. Don't ask me where the folks picked up a word like that. Maybe from the Confederates. Anyhow, it seems Tyrone was always up for a real bust and kept a few of the locals hanging out on stoops and rooftops. If anybody looking like a cop—or even looking like me—turned up, Tyrone knew it before you could blow a whistle and call in the cars. But now I knew what Tyrone didn't know I knew. Sweet Lord, gimme good intelligence, and I'll take care of the rest myself.

I can still go up a drainpipe as fast as I could when I was eighteen. I don't say I'm as good at the top as I was, but I can get there. This time, I had a few minutes to get my wind back. Then I started hiking across the roof real slow and easy. Sure enough, down at the far end this kid was lying half awake, half asleep, looking over the side down toward the street with an old .22 bolt-action rifle beside him. If he'd been in my unit, I'd have busted him down to buck private, taken away three months' pay, and let him rest up in the stockade for a while.

Never mind. I got nothing against it being easy. I hunkered down behind him and tucked my .357 Magnum up behind his ear.

—You want to show me where old Tyrone is taking his rest, son?

—Fuck you.

I slapped him on the chin with the front sight. He looked at the blood on his hand like he'd never seen any before. At least not his own.

—Now I can't show you what your brains look like, 'cause you're gonna be dead. But they're gonna be out there on the tar and cinders with people walking in 'em.

He understood that, and allowed as how he'd as soon help me as not. In fact, if I was bound and determined to knock off Tyrone and steal his stash, he could drive the truck. He had been looking to better himself in the business, and this looked like it might be his main chance. Truck, I thought. Truck? What the hell has he got going down there?

The boy led me down the roof stairs and along a hallway and about halfway down another set of stairs. Even in October, it was so hot I didn't think I was going to see the bottom. I damned near didn't, but it wasn't the heat. Shit, I *was* the heat.

Which is what the kid started yelling as he vaulted over the rail and went running down the dark hall before I could even draw a bead on him. He barely got out of range when some smoke stepped out of a doorway. I couldn't make out what he was carrying, but it made an awful lot of noise, and the stair rail next to my left hand disintegrated.

CHAPTER

6

I crouched down rubbing a numb hand, and squinted so I could see just where my shooter was hanging out. The window at the foot of the stairs was dirty, but I could see a doorframe just off to the left of the window. I could even see that the door opened away from me, toward the window. Just then, I heard steps. Nobody running. More like a fool thinking he was moving too easy to be heard, trying to mousetrap me. I aimed the Magnum right where the door crack had to be. Then I rolled the cylinder up one notch and pulled the trigger. I had got some people's attention.

When I pushed the door open, the punk wearing some kind of hosiery on his head had a hole in the front of his throat and one out the back. He wasn't dead yet, but he wouldn't be any more trouble. I kicked his shotgun across the room and made for the window.

So help me God, there was a rope ladder went down a floor, and at the bottom three guys were pushing cardboard boxes into the back of a new van as fast as they could. One of them was Tyrone. About as wide as he was tall, black as Sally Marshall's gumbo, and sweating like it was mid-July. I had found my man—and that truck the kid had mentioned, too.

—Hey, Tyrone, I called down, cocking my piece. —Remember like we used to say? Up against the wall, motherfucker...

See, every time I get to doing dramatics, I wish later I hadn't. If I'd just shot the sonofabitch in the ass, I could have saved myself a lot of trouble. But no. Tyrone looked up at me, then he looked across at the next building, and all of a sudden I'm caught in a downpour of glass and birdshot. Seems I'd forgotten Tyrone's *other* pickets. Thank God they favored shotguns. And number-eight shot.

I managed to get my arm over the window and squeeze off a shot into the hood of the car before they pulled away, but I knew it wasn't any good. I alternate wad-cutters and armor-piercing rounds in my .357. I used an AP for the punk at the door. So that shot over the window ledge didn't tear anything up. It just spattered on the engine block.

After I shook off the glass and picked up the shotgun and the box of shells lying on the floor, I made it out of there as fast as I could. Spotting that purple and gold van wasn't gonna be too hard. If I got down on the street fast enough. I hit the hall running.

It was easier picking up on Tyrone than I'd reckoned. On the way out toward Louisa Street, he'd hit a lady's shopping cart and run a kid on a bicycle into a bench at a bus stop. Go it, Tyrone. Every little bit helps.

I came barreling up onto the freeway, and sure enough old Ty was tooling along about eighty-five in toward the city. The traffic was medium, and he was flushing drivers out of the way pretty good till he come up the inside lane behind a big silver-blue pickup with tires

like a tractor, a Confederate flag glazed on the back
window, racing stripes, great big lights mounted on a
bar above the cab, and some bird dogs in back. What
with a couple of sixteen-wheelers on his right, Tyrone
didn't have any place to go, and the man in the pickup
seemed to think fifty-five was a fine speed. You could
see he was coming home from hunting, not going.

So Tyrone honked and honked as I was zipping up
behind him. The gentleman in the pickup kind of stood
on his rights, knowing he was going the speed limit
and nobody had a good legal reason in the world to
hassle him. After a few more honks, an arm came out
of the driver's window and lifted a finger to Tyrone. I
could read that prime honky's mind. Nigger in a brand-
new van. I'll be in hell on a long vacation before I move
over for that burr. There's times and circumstances in
this life where a black man can come to love a redneck
sonofabitch.

But Ty couldn't appreciate cracker pride. No, he meant
to be around that bastard and away. So he rammed his
bumper into the back of the truck. I was almost close
enough to take a shot at him, but the traffic was building
so I reckoned I'd better hold off and see what was going
down. When Tyrone slammed into the back of the pickup,
it jolted forward maybe five yards. Then that redneck hit
his brakes.

It wasn't a bad move on a warm day. Because, like a
lot of our Louisiana country boys, my head honky up
there had him a reinforced bumper in back made out of
a railroad tie. You could nudge him, but you weren't
gonna shove him around. Probably better you leave him
alone altogether—unless you had cutting and shooting
business in mind.

Tyrone's van just piled into him and lost most of its
front end. Whoever was driving the van must have felt

that engine beginning to nuzzle its way through the fire wall and back onto his lap. Then my cracker put the pedal to the metal on that pickup of his and went right back into position in the left lane—with big trucks in the other two lanes.

By then, I was on the van's ass. I still didn't want to take a shot because in the cycle of things the next bullet up in my pistol was another AP. A bad snap and it could go right through Tyrone's little business and hit my honorary deputy in the pickup.

One of the dudes in Tyrone's van decided to end the bullshit. He leaned way out the passenger window with somebody inside holding his legs and let go with something that looked like an old-fashioned pirate pistol. It took out the right side of that Confederate battle flag. I mean, the Stars and Bars vanished right in front of my eyes. If my pickup driver had a passenger, he was likely smeared all over the dashboard.

That pissed me off. Tyrone had a right to put some space between us if he could, but shooting double-naught buckshot at folks on the Interstate was a whole 'nother thing. I whipped out to the right, hit my throttle, and came up alongside the van just as that handkerchief-head started back inside with his sawed-off shotgun. He had too far to go. He didn't make it. I had my Magnum in my left hand, and I hit him hard with the barrel right where his ear met his scalp. The shotgun dropped and sent up sparks from the pavement, then whoever was inside let go, and the gunner went down to the cement after it. Behind us, I could hear the cars hitting their brakes. Too late.

My honky wasn't cruising along waiting for the next salvo, either. He'd whipped over to his right, sideswiping the trailer truck in the next lane. If you were a damned fool, you might think he'd learned his lesson and was trying to give Tyrone and his geeks all the room they needed. I knew better than that, but whoever was driving Tyrone's van didn't. He punched his gas to the floor and took off around the left of the pickup. Maybe I should say that was his plan. He got up about even with the pickup when my bird-hunting man came back into the lane full tilt, pushing the van into a concrete retaining wall on the left.

It was like the Fourth of July. Sparks and pieces of body steel and a sound like somebody was cutting the damned van in half with a chain saw. I was hoping the folks driving the freeway behind had figured out that this wasn't a bunch of old boys cut loose from a convention down at the Rivergate, because it was gonna get worse before it got better.

It did. Just ahead, you had a cutoff. The inside lane ran down to Claiborne Avenue, and from there right into the University section of town. What was left on the van just skittered off the wall and took that exit like it saw a repair shop down at the end of the line.

About then it occurred to me my redneck might not realize whose side I was on. I reached down and grabbed my red sparkler and slapped it on the roof of the car. Then I gave the siren a turn or two as the pickup and I both sailed on past the Claiborne exit.

The pickup knew he'd be halfway to Causeway before he could get off if he kept going the way he was going, so he hit his brakes again as he spun his wheel, and did a really fine 180° right in the middle of the freeway. He came back at me, and I saw him for the first time.

Red hair and beard, some kind of baseball-style cap that said the name of his tribe, Evinrude, on the front, and crazy eyes set about two centimeters apart behind a big veined nose. I knew he could see my light and hear my siren. I also knew he didn't give a flying fuck. You get one of these Caucasian critters charged, and he goes till he's done or dropped.

Cars behind us were skidding, piling into one another, trying to get out of our way as I did my little quick turn just like the cracker. He went back to the exit and smashed his fender getting down onto it, causing some lady in a Chrysler New Yorker convertible that still had a dealer tag to fan out and run into a panel truck that said Herbert Refrigeration on the side. I went right behind him.

We went through a red light at Melpomene one-two, with folks running up on the curb or over the esplanade that goes down the center of Claiborne. I could see up ahead that the traffic was bunched up around Toledano Street, and that Tyrone's wreck was barely making speed anyhow. I figured that lane-switching maneuver the country boy made had likely sliced the left front tire off the van.

Sure enough, a block farther down, and it was up on the esplanade for the van and time to bail out. I thought it was funny. I enjoyed it anyhow, but some folks say I've got a mean streak.

There was Tyrone and two other guys coming out of their van, trying to carry cardboard boxes with them. I understood how they felt. If they were toting cocaine in those boxes, they might have a million bucks' worth of supply there. It's hard to leave your inventory behind when circumstances move you along, and too late for a closeout sale.

Never mind me. They weren't gonna make it anyhow. As they headed across the wide grass of the esplanade, that silver-blue pickup bounced over the curb and started bearing down on the one behind who was trying to carry three good-sized boxes. The doper looked around just in time to see the wages of sin up close. Eight cylinders and a winch on the front. The truck hit him, dropped him, passed over him, and kept right on rolling for the next one, leaving the first guy all curled up, looking like he'd got caught in the middle of a blizzard on a hot autumn day in New Orleans. The grass was plastered with coke for ten or fifteen feet around him. I expected the neighbors would come scratch themselves up a toke or two before I got back.

By then, number two was down in the street on the far side amidst paused amazed traffic, thrashing around like a crab with his claw up his ass, and he was covered with white powder, too. This was gonna be some spectacular bust. I hated that I was gonna have to share credit with this citizen in the pickup, but fair is fair.

I saw Tyrone losing boxes as he tried to keep running, and I could see about where the pickup was gonna intersect with him. If I wanted any small talk with old Ty, I was gonna have to start playing copper instead of interested witness. I drove across the esplanade and the inbound lanes of Claiborne just as Tyrone dropped the last of his stash and tried to get the pumps of a filling station between him and the redneck. It wasn't a bad move, considering he didn't have any others, but it didn't take him far. The pickup slid to a stop, and the guy with the red hair and beard came out with a pump gun. He was in a hurry, and his first shot hit the cement right in front of Tyrone and glanced up, hitting him in the legs. Tyrone was screaming for the brothers who worked in the station, but the brothers were down behind a pile of tires on sale, and they weren't coming out till the whole scene got changed.

My hunting man levered his pump and then pointed it right at Tyrone's big quivering belly just as I skidded onto the station concrete, came out of the car, and leaned over the hood with my Magnum in one hand and my badge in the other.

—Hold it, police, I yelled. —You got all the other ones. I need that one.

The cracker turned real slow. I had all the right in the world to shoot him, but I was damned if I was going to. He was still crazy mad, and I hadn't seen into his cab. For all I knew, Tyrone and the rest of those assholes had killed his best friend. I knew one more thing. That gun was full of birdshot. It wasn't going to come through my car and hit me, so I could give my good buddy a moment or two to cool down. He was staring at me then, like he was trying to make out what I wanted, what I was doing there aiming a pistol at him. For his sake, I sure hoped he could distinguish between one black face and the next. I didn't want to kill him, but I wanted a whole lot less for him to kill me. It was in his court.

It seemed like a work week and a long holiday as I waited for him to make up his mind. I could hear Tyrone reciting the Hail Mary and getting into an Act of Contrition just like they'd taught us at parochial school a long time ago. I could hear police sirens zeroing in on us from all over. Lord God, I did want this thing shut down and Tyrone in bracelets before the street fuzz gathered. My redneck's chances were gonna go way down if a bunch of cruisers started sliding up around the station and they saw him with a shotgun aimed at me.

—You the one cold-cocked that nigger bastard who blew out my rear window?

—That's me, I said. —Captain Ralph Trapp, NOPD.

—You say you got to have this one? he asked me.

—I do. I really do. If I didn't...

He nodded, lowered the pump gun, and walked back to his truck. He set the shotgun against his quarter-panel and sat down on the running board and started crying very softly. You couldn't hear him. You just knew from the way his shoulders moved, the way he was covering his face with his hands. I looked over at Tyrone.

—Move, you tub of guts, and I'll blow you a new asshole, hear?

I don't know if he heard or not, but he was kneeling in his own blood on those bad legs and had gotten on to another prayer that seemed to fit pretty good.

—St. Michael the archangel, defend us in battle...

I walked over to the cracker and put my hand on his shoulder. I just couldn't look into that truck cab right away. When I finished talking to Tyrone, I was gonna see if I could get him fried.

—They've done killed her, the redheaded man was sobbing. —They've done killed Daisy. She was the best thing ever happened to me...

Oh, shit, I thought. They've killed his wife.

—I'm sorry, I told him. —But they're gonna pay.

—Pay what? You can't save her, can't bring her back.

He rose up then, and I saw he was as tall as I am. He leaned into the cab, and his fingers got lost in the blood on the passenger side. I looked then, and I understood how he felt.

—I had her since she was three weeks old. Her momma died, and I weaned her myself.

There on the Naugahyde seat lay an old hound bitch. She must have been past fifteen years old, and she had shriveled and turned gray around the muzzle. Some of the buckshot had caught her in the back of the head and right shoulder, and the seat was covered with her blood. As I looked, she shivered and the light went out of her eyes. I remember thinking two things: she'd spent her last day hunting with this old boy who was surely the love of her life—and what a goddamned shame it was the law didn't count her killing murder.

•   •   •

When the boys were writing it up, I lied a little. I told them I'd asked Gene A. Downey to help me out. I believe all the TV people crowding around him, me saying he was a hero, helped a little. After the ambulance crews had harvested Tyrone and his two flunkies, I made them put Daisy into a body bag.

—Them bags cost, the orderly was telling me.

—I'll pay, I said. —Stop being a horse's ass.

I gave him one of my cards, and walked back to the car. I expected it was about time to check in downtown.

As I walked to my car, I stopped by Gene Downey. —They put Daisy up in the back of the truck, I told him. He nodded, all put back together by then, sunburned, stoic, likely wanting a Dixie beer in a long-neck bottle.

—Glad I could help you, he said. —If they busts out, gimme a call, will you?

I laughed and shook his outstretched hand. —Will I ever...

Down at Tulane and Broad, I parked and walked into Central Lockup. It was gonna be a long night if I could make it that way. Tyrone knew a lot I wanted to know, and I had him on a list of charges that could keep him paying lawyers for twenty years. I was ready to start in on him when an administrative clerk stopped me.

—Major Mauvais wants to see you, Captain.

Mauvais is sixty or thereabouts and joined the force when, if you were a black officer, you didn't arrest a white man no matter what he was doing. If a white man was shooting kids in a schoolyard, Mauvais and his generation went and called for a white cop to come make him stop. It wasn't a department policy you could find written anywhere. It was just understood. No need starting a riot back in 1948 or thereabouts.

Those days had left a mark on all the blacks who had gotten shoved up after the Movement started. They were grades over where they ever reckoned to be, and they sure as hell didn't want any kind of trouble that might cost them even a grim look from the whites at the very top echelon—and even when they *were* the top echelon, they still kept looking behind them. Some men you can't knock the chains off of. The links are still in place whether you see them or not. It was as if they resented the rest of us who'd come in with military training or after a career in the FBI or Secret Service or even out of the academy. All the old bastards ever had to say to me was, Ease Off.

Mauvais was sitting behind his desk in a dark gray suit with his dark gray hair and his dark gray face that he couldn't quite wipe the accommodating smile off of even when he was dressing down one of the ranks. The sonofabitch couldn't help looking like a parking attendant going for the Big Tip. We've all got our lots in life, I thought. Mauvais wears a nice gold leaf on his shoulder tabs, but he's still shoveling shit for the Man.

Somebody was gabbing with Mauvais. It was one of his staff people, and he was going on like paratroopers had hit City Hall. Seems word about how I brought Tyrone in had just filtered up. Mauvais looked up and saw me.

—Goddamned crazy bastard, Major Mauvais started off, and for the very first time I could remember, that shit-eating smile of his was nowhere to be seen.

The meeting went on till dark. Major Tyndall from Narcotics and a couple of feds I'd never come across joined us. Tyndall seemed to be asking permission to lynch me down in Jackson Square, and Mauvais was leaning that way. He was talking about civil service hearings, bringing me up on charges, reduction in rank, all kinds of horse-shit.

I sat listening with my mind other places. Hell, I'd stood three court-martials in ten years and beaten the piss out of all of 'em. I'm too old and been reamed too many times for a little chickenshit civil service hearing to sweat me.

Tyndall, a big pasty-faced dude from Alabama, was getting into chain of command and proper channels and me losing a witness to a shooter—all the crap you use when you don't know how to do your own job. He still had a hard-on about how I walked around him on the Burnucci indictments. About halfway through, somebody turned on the TV to see how they were going to play my little scrimmage on the six o'clock news.

It was so fine. I just sat there and watched. See, like I said, the media can be a pain in the ass. But when they get hold of a Lone Ranger story, they're gonna play it till it rolls over and dies. The worst thing they said was Captain Ralph Trapp had broken the back of a dope ring operating out of Desire project, had turned up cocaine with a street value of nearly two million dollars, and had arrested, with the help of a courageous private citizen, a notorious leader of black crime in the city.

There was old Gene A. Downey standing by his pickup, like he was anchor on *Newscene 9*, telling how it had been. He allowed as how he'd never had a whole hell of a lot of use for nigger—oops!—black cops, but Captain Ralph Trapp had changed his mind. Then he got teary and kind of drifted into telling about Daisy, and how I'd gotten the body bag for her and paid for it myself.

It went on like that with pictures of ambulances being

loaded out at the project, ambulances being loaded on the I-10, ambulances being loaded on Claiborne Avenue. The final count was three dead, three all tore to hell, and nine arrests pending—which took into account the rest of Tyrone's pickets and pushers back in the project.

I didn't say anything. Not even when Gwen Daly of *Newscene 9* summed up, saying the world must be changing for the better when a black cop and a redneck in a pickup join forces to protect and to serve.

Nobody else said anything, either. There were broken hearts in that room, and the civil service was gonna be out one hearing. Mauvais looked at Tyndall and shrugged.

—What you gonna do? he asked.

—Surely you have internal procedures, one of the feds popped up. He was a little sawed-off honky with glasses and a Gucci briefcase his momma probably bought him. You see one of those dips, and you know just how fine Gene A. Downey and his kin really are—warts and all.

Tyndall kept looking at me like he was sizing my neck for a rope. —That's right. Internal procedures. Trapp can't walk in on my bust like that. We've been...

The fed started talking over him. —We've been taping Jefferson and his crowd for months. One of the men killed was feeding us information.

When he said "taping," I grinned at Mauvais. He just stared at the ceiling, and I knew I was off the hook. Internal procedures and all.

When it was over, Tyndall stopped me in the hall.

—You stay the hell off my cases, Trapp. If it goes down this way again...

—... You'll be looking for a job, I told him. —Quit

fucking with the feds. Go in there and chew ass. You could have had Tyrone two years ago if you'd just gone calling—instead of *taping.*

—Why the hell did you do it? the little fed wanted to know. —There are ways to do things...

I stared him down. —Tell your momma to come pick up her clothes. I'm tired of her, I said.

The other fed almost laughed out loud.

—Trapp..., Tyndall started.

—Tyrone's got information on a case I'm working, I said, cutting him off. —I didn't give a shit about the dope. I just wanted to question him. When he saw me, he lit out for the woods. It just came down that way.

—Don't let it come down that way again, Tyndall rasped, giving me the hardest eyes he had.

I kind of grinned at him, then started walking away.

—What's *your* momma doing nights, Tyndall? I said over my shoulder.

When I looked back from the end of the hall, the feds had hold of him by his shoulders trying to talk sense, and I believe he was scandalizing my name.

I was sipping a polystyrene cup full of good black coffee when they brought Tyrone in. He wasn't looking too spry, but then he never had. He had a bandage on his head, and they'd made shorts out of his hundred-and-fifty-dollar slacks so they could tape up the birdshot wounds where Gene A. Downey had popped him. I had this bad feeling right up front. I didn't like the expression on his face.

Tyrone was looking to come out of prison an old man shuffling around in loose shoes without an appetite left to his name if half the charges we had pasted on him stuck. But he looked like we were getting together for lunch. No pain, no strain. Tyrone knew the streets, but he wasn't that cool. Unless he had himself a sure pass out of stir.

—Well, lookee here, I started. —It's little Tyrone Jefferson all busted to shit. What happened, brother?

—What you say, Rat, he smiled, as if I was his goddamned defense attorney. —If you'd called ahead, we could have had us a nice talk without all that mess on the freeway.

I laughed. —The only mess on the freeway was your gunner after ten or fifteen cars ran him over.

He shook his head. —That boy Archie? What a waste. I was gonna see him on a scholarship through college.

—He may make Tulane Med School yet . . . if nobody claims the body.

Tyrone shook his head. —How come you got it in for me? he asked. —I mean, brother, we went to school together.

—Never mind that, I said. —You want to talk now or wait for your shyster?

—Man, I got nothing to hide. I'm a hard-working man.

—I hope you know about busting rocks.

—It ain't gonna come to that. I never been convicted of nothing but that little prescription rap.

—Let's talk about what we're looking at up front. Possession with intent to distribute, attempted murder, assault with a deadly weapon. They may even rig a couple of felony murder raps on account of those poor bastards who checked out working for you.

Tyrone nodded, spread his hands on the tabletop. —And you're gonna walk me right on out if I give you something? Right? What you want?

When I went into Desire, my mind was on Peetie, but some unconscious hunch made me ask, —Why'd you mix it up with Danny Bynum?

—Who?

I didn't answer. I just sat and waited.

—Oh, yeah. That kid with the band. That little nigger come preaching over to the project like he was Jesus.

—Bad for business? Bad enough you wanted him off?

—I heard he collapsed, but I never done him nothing.

—OD'ed. Speedball. Heroin and coke in DMSO.

Tyrone was real convincing. —What? he asked. —DMSO? You serious?

—You know what it is?

—Sure, brother. You forgetting I was a licensed pharmacist?

—I'm not forgetting. I figure you'd know where to come by it.

—The little bastard come from the coast, didn't he? They sell it everywhere out there. Even some filling stations got it. I'll be damned. That motherfucker was some big-time hypocrite. I would've sworn he was clean.

So much for Camille's theory and hunches. Now for some police work.

—Okay, forget Bynum. Who hit Peetie Postum?

—That witness you got blowed away? Tyrone grinned and shook his head. —Brothers on the street been calling it a hunting accident.

—I'm gonna be talking to the assistant DA. I can build you up or tear you down. Same way when I testify in court. Facts don't change, but I can lean different ways, you know.

Tyrone's lower lip drooped, and he worked up some wrinkles in his forehead. Wasn't any need in me going on. He knew all right. That's why he was talking to me without his lawyer.

—I tell you what, Tyrone said. —I don't have nothing on this business with Postum. But I know a lot of people. Maybe I could find something out.

—That'd do, I said. —But don't wrap up three pounds of bullshit in a one-pound sack, I told him. —I got all I need for the garden.

Tyrone smiled at me. I couldn't make out just what he was smiling about, but I walked out of the interrogation room a lot less sure of where I was at than when I'd walked in.

CHAPTER
7

Next morning, I ran till my tongue hung out, and decided I'd catch myself some breakfast down in the coffee shop at the Pontchartrain Hotel. It's the Uptown power station when you're talking politics or law or finance in New Orleans. You find city councilmen and federal judges, big-time contractors and every other manner of critter that moves and shakes around town. Nothing fancy about it. It's just been in the right location a long, long time, and people gravitated to it. Institutions are like that. I remember an old black funeral-home owner who had made himself a few million back in segregation days. He told me once, "I didn't give a damn about joining Rex or eating at Antoine's, but I did dearly want to take my morning grits at the Pontchartrain Coffee Shop, 'cause that's where it all got done."

On the way there, I passed Smith's Records and pulled my car to a stop. I wanted to hear Danny Bynum sing "Wise Child" again. I bought the record, and when I saw his face smiling up at me, I almost lost interest in breakfast.

But I reckoned on a long day ahead, so I went in and took a table near the front windows. While I was waiting for my eggs and bacon and grits and biscuits, I read the liner notes on the record album. Nothing but the usual hype about some rootless kids in a California high school finding there was one thing they did very well: make music. Not one of them had been born in the Golden State. You could call them internal refugees. From Oklahoma, New Jersey, Kansas, Oregon and, yes, Louisiana.

But amidst all the adjectives and breathless chatter, I couldn't help noticing one thing: nothing was said about where the band had gotten its name. I guess Desire Project sounded like one more step in the sexual revolution, and the record producers were happy to let it stand just that way. Valley Girls and Beach Boys wouldn't want to know anything about the kind of Desire project Danny had had in mind. On the other hand, probably Danny didn't know either. It must have been just a name to him, a place his mother mentioned now and then, something from the past that she might even have conjured up with fondness. People can do that. On a cold day they can look back at hell and remember how warm it was.

As I was eating, Larry Lawrence stopped at the table. He's a state representative, and Desire is part of his district. He spends a lot of time sobbing about more police presence in the projects. But then Larry is full of shit.

—Say, Rat, I hear you been busy.

—Same old store, Larry. Every now and again, we have us a fire sale.

He wasn't sure whether to laugh or not. Half of his constituents are old folks and women getting cut and whipped and jerked around all the time. The other half is the cutters and whippers and jerkers. It keeps him nervous. Even Larry hasn't figured a way to attack violence one day and speak out forcefully in favor of street crime the next.

—Well, we got to break up the dope traffic. It's a killer.

—Yeah, I knew you'd feel that way. What'd Tyrone put into your last campaign, brother?

He tried to smile, but it reminded me of Mauvais's heartrending attempts. Nothing honest in it.

—Well, now, with respect, Rat, Tyrone's got a trial coming, don't he? I mean, innocent till...

—Can it, Larry. You saw the TV. The sonofabitch was running across Claiborne Avenue with six or eight pounds of coke in cardboard boxes when Gene Downey and I pulled his string and broke his play.

—Yeah, well, that's too bad. Ty's got good qualities.

—He passed on a couple hundred thousand of 'em to you the last time you ran, huh?

Larry gave me this sly appreciative look.

—Rat, you got yourself a name now. Good TV exposure. I could use a man like you.

—That's what the women all tell me.

—Politics is where it's at, dude.

—I know. But they won't give me a warrant to go in and clean it out.

I think his laugh was sincere that time.

—Man, don't you like good things?

—Love 'em. Can't get enough.

—Then come on over. Take you an early retirement from NOPD and jump right in. I could run you against Walt Roppolo Uptown here. Blacks see you're black, and the white folks think you're Captain Midnight.

—Larry, if I came on over and and jumped right in, I'd slide on the pigshit and break my leg.

I laid a ten-dollar bill on top of my check and got up.

—Don't take the money, Larry. It's for the waitress.

•   •   •

I drove down to Sacre Coeur then. I had to see Camille and offer her whatever ease I could. You never get quite past that first love. It doesn't run the rest of your life, and maybe you wouldn't even want it back, but it's there like a faint penciled circle on a dusty old map, and sometimes, when things are bad or even when they're good, you find yourself looking back to that location in your heart. Just like you'd never left.

It wasn't that I had in mind to grab hold and try to pull the past into the present. It wasn't the time for that, and anyhow, Camille and I were different people from the kids we'd been. Still, on the elevator going up to the fourth floor, it was as if I could taste her lips on mine again. It seemed I could close my eyes and we'd be walking down Rampart Street on a Saturday afternoon or on the levee in darkness watching the ships coming and going on the river, their lights reflecting like stars in the water, the two of us wondering if one of them was ours.

When I reached the door of Danny's suite, I looked down the hall toward the door of Burnucci's. Sure enough, one of the Bookends was leaning up against the wall like a cigar-store Indian in a two-hundred-and-fifty-dollar suit. When he saw me, I believe he turned a whiter shade of pale. I knew he wasn't carrying. And he knew I knew. His piece was inside the room with number two or number one. Whichever one he wasn't. I smiled at him like a good neighbor and knocked on Danny's door.

Camille answered, and I almost started talking. But then, behind her, over by the big window that looked out on the town, I saw somebody staring at me across her shoulder. The light was coming through the window behind him and his face was in shadow, but I was sure I knew who it was. I'd seen enough of the sonofabitch in the last couple of months. But I told myself, no, it couldn't be. I mean, suppose you were in Timbuktu, amongst the natives, and all of a sudden the old family doctor appears on the street. It's hard to believe what you don't expect, can't even imagine seeing in some certain place—even a circle on a map scratched in your heart.

It was Nick Burnucci, all right. He didn't look out of place or uncomfortable about me finding him with Camille. He just stood there like he was paying for the suite, and all of a sudden, in a single moment, I filled in twenty years of wondering.

—Goddamn, I said, not in anger or because Burnucci was standing there, but because right then I knew whose white Cadillac had hummed its way into Desire and taken Camille out of my life. All that old buried emotion came back strong—but distant, like it wasn't something that had happened to me at all, but to some other poor bastard who had deserved better, who hadn't known how to move out of the way when the Honky Express was coming through.

Burnucci pulled together a mean smile from somewhere. It said, *My people nearly took you out along with Peetie the other morning, and if I make a couple of calls, push the right button, you'd be shipped to Algiers or Gentilly to investigate dirty bookstores. I'm still in the white Cadillac and you're still sitting on the stoop with a handkerchief wrapped around your head. Keep it in mind. It's like physics. It don't change, darkie.* He had a pretty good style. He held that stare for maybe five seconds, then he stepped up behind Camille, touched her like his hand and her shoulder were a matched set.

—I'll drop back by later, Mrs. Bynum, he said. —Best of luck with the boy.

I moved out of the way and let him pass. The Express route was still passing right over me. I hadn't got myself together just yet. The last time I'd seen a look like Nick Burnucci's it had been on the face of a KGB man in West

Berlin—just before I blew his face up against a basement wall, smile and all.

Camille wasn't slow. She knew. As Nick passed out of the room, she'd walked away from me. Now she'd taken Nick's place standing by the window. Still in shadow.

—Jesus, I said. —It was . . . him.

—Let it go, Ralph. Anybody who remembers twenty years ago must run an antique shop.

—All of a sudden, it feels like twenty minutes.

—Twenty. Years. Okay?

—So he took you out of the project and made you his lady?

She laughed harshly. —His . . . lady? Not exactly. I can't remember him taking me home to meet Dad.

—You belonged to him, and Danny's his son.

—No.

—No wonder the kid doesn't know his father. And no wonder you never told him anything.

—That's not true. That's not why.

—Bullshit. That's why Tyrone was mouthing off about you out at the project. That's what got Danny crossed up with him.

—No, no, no. If you've got to know the truth . . .

—Don't bother. I can guess what that'd sound like. Nick peddled you around when he got enough of it, didn't he? You must've made all the conventions in town afterward.

—Get out, she almost screamed at me. —Get out. I'm not going to tell you a damned thing. You think you know what . . .

—I *do* know. After twenty years wondering, I finally know.

I took a hike then. There was nothing more for me to say. Nothing for *us* to say. Whatever bad news she had coming now, she'd have to handle it the same way she'd handled the last twenty years. It wasn't my game anymore.

As I pulled the door closed and looked down the hall, I saw Burnucci talking to Bookend. Nick tried that stare of his again. I didn't like it worth a shit, so I thought maybe I'd pop him back.

—Dropped by to see how your son is doing, Nicky-babe?

I didn't expect what I got. Nick's face sagged as if I'd slugged him in the gut, as if he was aging right there in front of me. He started to say something but it wouldn't come. Then he stepped back unsteadily and vanished into his old man's suite with Bookend right behind.

I looked after him, surprised. Maybe he didn't know about Camille and me. Why should he? It hadn't been anything personal for him. He'd just seen a fine piece of black twat and taken it off the shelf. I'd been less than a dark blank place in those days. Just a kid with a little job in a seafood market and half a handful of hopes. Or maybe it got up under his lower ribs for me to be talking family business just like I'd seen the birth certificate.

I walked down to the waiting room and sat down on one of the love seats, trying to clear my head and ease my mind. Camille was right. I wasn't dealing antiques, so why had it hit me so hard? If it hadn't been Nick Burnucci, it had to have been somebody. Why should finding out about something twenty years gone make me feel like a gutted catfish? Wes Colvin was always quoting somebody, saying, *The past isn't dead. It isn't even past.* Something to that, I thought as I got up and started down toward the elevators. Carrying the truth like an ancient burden, all the old dreams fading back into history again.

I was about to push the button when I turned and looked over at the nurses' station. One nurse was sitting filling in forms, and behind her rose a set of monitors, little TV screens that zeroed in on the patients' beds so the people at the station could see what was happening in the rooms even if some of the bells and whistles on the machines failed to go off when they should.

On one screen I saw Danny Bynum lying as if he was dreaming of being on TV with his daddy—and on the next one there was Nick and his old man. Nick seemed upset and was gesturing, talking fast. The old man was trying to calm him down. Mr. X looked like he was losing the argument.

It occurred to me how much I'd like to have myself a tape with audio of what I was seeing just then. My hand pushed the elevator button without my telling it to, and the car doors opening said it was time to move on. Just as I backed into the elevator, my eyes still on the screens, I saw old man Burnucci picking up the phone and dialing. It had to be trouble for somebody. I wished to hell I knew who.

I met Wes and Denise at La Louisiane for lunch. It used to be called Moran's, though nobody with Irish blood ever stood behind a counter. Denise says the fettuccine Alfredo is better than the original in Rome. I can't argue with her. The only time I went to Rome was to cripple a Syrian, and we had to get out in a hurry afterward.

Denise gave me a sly look.

—I suppose you know they're calling you El Supremo over in the DA's office. One of the deputy assistants said if we could clone you, we wouldn't need criminal court.

I laughed. It's not a bad reputation to have. You get what you need easier, and people tend to leave you alone. I never could figure why the old gunfighters liked to bitch about their reputations. I've worked hard on mine.

Wes had his face in his drink trying not to laugh.

—The print media missed again. I'm gonna get a phone in my car so you can call me next time you're about to . . . do something wonderful.

He lost it then and roared with laughter. —Shit, I don't think I can stand it. El Supremo . . .

When something amuses him, Wes is not quiet. People at the other tables turned toward us. One guy started pointing at me, telling his girlfriend something.

—Wes, Denise cut him short, —please?

—I can't help it. My writing has created a monster.

He was talking about a little feature he'd written on me for the Sunday supplement of the *Item* a while back. It had gone on about some of my cases, and made a lot out of how I was always dressed like a diplomat. By and large, he told the truth, but I thought the line about creating me was a little strong. I'd always had in mind to do that for myself.

—I just went out to the project to talk to Tyrone, I started.

Wes's eyes got big. —Three guys dead, three in the hospital, nine headed for the can . . . and you just wanted to *talk* to some jig . . . oops, I mean some guy.

—Tyrone *is* a jig, I told him. —The sonofabitch sells shit to kids. He's almost lowlife enough to be a redneck.

It didn't help. Wes had hold of me where I live, and he wanted to shake it a little. —I got this picture of what happens when you go to *yell* at somebody. Buildings collapse, planes fall out of the sky, animals turn queer . . .

I couldn't help laughing. —You want me to come up to the paper ready to *whip* somebody?

—God forbid, he said, making big eyes at Denise.

—Let me know if you want to do a deal with Jefferson, Denise told me. —We've got enough to put him away for fifty real-time years.

I laughed. We've all picked up that piece of computer

talk. What's a real-time year? That's a year with three hundred sixty-five and a quarter days in it that some sleazy bastard has to serve—as opposed to ordinary years with good time taken off and probation and clemency and commutation and the rest of the crap hoods buy from politicians one way or the other.

—Youall ready to drop some of the charges if I can get him off the dime and talking about the Peetie Postum hit?

Denise nodded. —You can tell him we'll give it a lot of thought.

Wes looked from one of us to the other. We both smiled at him like he was the odd man out. —You guys are fixing to shove it to Jefferson, aren't you?

—Not at all, Denise said in a smooth syrupy voice. —I'll do any deal Rat wants—on possession, attempted murder, resisting arrest...

—There's something else, Wes said suspiciously.

—There's at least ten real-time years for income tax evasion, she smiled. —The feds moved in after Rat's visit. They found money and all kinds of records out at Desire. Tyrone had his aunt keeping his books. The feds have everything they need for a conviction.

It didn't make my day, but it gave me some slack for playing with little Ty. I could walk him through eighty percent of the state stuff before the feds ever made him for taxes. I didn't give a shit which pocket the people kept him in, so long as he was in.

That settled, we concentrated on the food. The fettuccine was smooth as Black Jack and rainwater, and the lemon-butter shrimp finished things off just fine.

—Did you talk to Camille today? Denise asked over coffee.

—Funny you should ask, I said. —Not exactly. We yelled at each other a little.

—Rat, why...?

I told her why. Denise looked startled. —You really believe Nick Burnucci...I mean, did he admit anything? What did he say?

—He looked like I'd hit him in the belly with a night-stick. For just a minute, it all went away on him. Look, honey, I saw it in his face. I saw it in hers. When you know something, you know it, don't you?

Denise looked away, pensive. She had her own memories.

—I guess you do, she said softly.

I told them about my little stop by the nurses' station, the Burnucci Show of Shows on that TV monitor.

—I'd give a pretty to hear what goes as family chitchat with those two, I said, —but it's silent movies, and I can't read lips.

Wes and I got to talking about how the Burnuccis were wired into the power circuit, and we didn't notice Denise sitting there sipping her coffee and thinking away. Then, all of a sudden, she broke in.

—You could, you know.

—Who could? Wes asked her. —Could what?

—Why, we could rig a video recorder to the nurses' monitor, and get a tape of whatever Mr. X and Nicky-babe are up to. With their track record, I'm sure I can get a warrant.

Wes laughed. —Then you show the old man your warrant, and stuff a bug in his nose to get sound to go with your pictures?

—Hold it, I said. —They got more machines and gadgets in there than a stereo shop. They're trying to make it look good for the court so they can hold on to that continuance.

Wes shrugged. —You really think somebody could slip in one more ding-dong unnoticed?

—How's Burnucci gonna know? A little camouflage, and...

Denise suddenly looked glum. —Can it. His doctor's Roy Panatella. He'd know—and he'd blow the whistle so quick...

Wes cut in, looking devilish. —I got it. Oh, sweet momma.

—What?

—You don't mike Burnucci's room. You mike the wall of the room next to his.

I grabbed him around the neck. —Now I know why I pay you so much.

He laughed. —Can I have an advance?

Denise nodded. —And with Danny Bynum's suite on the same floor, Rat can come and go without anyone hitting the alarm bell when he changes tapes in the recorder.

—If Camille Bynum will see him again, Wes said. —How's the weather forecast on that? he asked me.

—How about partly cloudy. I guess I'll know better next time I see her, I said.

It was late by the time I finished all the reports I had to file on the Jefferson arrest, but I was feeling a little better. Denise's phone call that she'd gotten the surveillance warrant had done it. Nobody could guarantee an ear on the Burnuccis was going to give us anything. Maybe what I wanted to hear had already gone down while I was watching at the nurses' station, deaf as a post. Or maybe father and son had been arguing about what kind of wine the old man wanted that evening. Still, it was a wedge. I had hold of a bunch of pieces that didn't come together, and I had to fill in somewhere.

I dropped by the CID and ordered the bug and recorder

installed at Sacre Coeur, then followed the tech to the hospital to make sure it was done carefully, without attracting any attention. Miking Burnucci's suite was important. The least it could do was blow a hole through his excuse for avoiding trial. The best was giving us information on who had set up Peetie's killing—and how they'd known just where and when. That was a lot to hope for, but it don't cost any more to hope for salvation than to wish for a two-buck cigar.

As I checked out the installation of the recorder at the nurses' station, I saw one of the Burnucci Bookends down the hall giving me the eye. He looked away when I stopped by the door to Danny's suite.

The way Camille and I had parted was on my mind as I started to knock. Maybe I should have called first. But the door gave way under my hand, and I had no choice but to step inside. The lights in the room were out, and the only illumination was from the glow of the city outside. Across the room, near the window, I could see a curl of cigarette smoke rising in the darkness. My eyes followed it down, and I saw the red glow pulsing bright, then fade.

—Camille, I said softly.

—Ralph, she answered, her voice brittle, dead, as far away as the cold Pacific.

—Listen, I was out of line. I'm sorry.

—No. I hurt you all that time ago. You had a right to hurt me back.

I walked through the shadows to her side. —I never wanted to hurt you back, I said. —Not then. Not now. Scores don't ever get evened out. People just get broken, tore up, dropped away like leaves off a tree.

—Did you feel then like I do now? Like somebody was going around through the world turning off the lights?

I took a deep breath, and remembered. What I'd felt was a little worse than that. When I heard about that white Cadillac coming to the project for Camille, I'd felt worthless. I was just one more little nigger boy who nobody had to take seriously. I didn't have anything, because anything I had was only by sufferance. If a white Cadillac wanted it, it wasn't gonna be mine anymore. Not a job, not a woman, not a place in the world.

—No, I told her. —The lights stayed on. Real bright, and they all seemed to be pointed at me. I ran.

—Ran?

—To the army, to Europe. To dirty little fights in alleys and basements in towns you never heard of. With people who deserved to be hurt. Fights I could win, and no lights at all.

—You must have been lonely.

—I don't remember that. I don't think so.

She rose from the chair and ground out the cigarette. Then she walked into the next room and stood by her boy's bed, stroking his dark hair.

—I'm afraid he may be leaving me ... the way I left you, she whispered.

I could feel her pain and some of my own. I've hurt and been hurt without a thought. But there's something deep, different in losing a child. The only death I ever came to hate and fear was this kind: the death of somebody young like Danny Bynum.

Camille stood tranced beside him for a moment. Then, as if she possessed some switch inside that she could throw when she had a mind, her head came up, her expression changed, and she walked back into the sitting room, turned on a table lamp, and started to pour whisky into two glasses.

—This is a nice hospital, she said. —Everyone is very

kind. You've been kind, too, Ralph, dropping by so often.

I couldn't let that lie. —There's something you should know, I started.

—What?

—I'm here tonight because Nick's father is a patient in this hospital. We just bugged his room.

—You want Nick? Camille said, her eyes on the big window, the silent pulsing red city outside.

—All right, but the old man more than him.

She turned back to me, her eyes cold points catching the light from the lamp.

—Franco . . . the old man.

I told her about what had gone down. I told her about Peetie Postum and how it ended in Baton Rouge. I couldn't tell if she was listening or not. By the time I was done, there was this funny little smile on her face.

—His name, his real name, is Dante, she said, as if answering a question I hadn't asked.

—Huh?

—Danny . . . Dante.

I could hear the Honky Express revving again, back there in the past. —I see, I answered, not seeing any more than I had to.

—No, you don't, Camille said, that smile unchanged. —You don't see at all, but that's all right. Then the smile faded, and she hit that switch inside again.

—I want to go in and stay with him now, she said. —Was there anything else?

—I don't think so, I answered, but before I finished the sentence, she'd stepped into the shadows of that other room, and I headed for the door.

CHAPTER
8

I didn't drive right home. The night was cool with that strange mild bite of coming autumn in the air. It felt like late summer in Germany when the days were long and warm, but beneath the warmth was that hint, that little prophecy that winter was on the way.

I went off the I-10 at Louisa Street and made a circuit out past the Desire project for no good reason at all. The names of the streets around it suddenly came into focus again for me.

It's hard to believe those names. I've wondered most of my life who made them up, and why. There's Treasure Street, and Abundance and Benefit. Humanity, Industry, and Pleasure Streets—all these in the midst of hopelessness and squalor and stone meanness out at the edge of what human beings can suffer, what they can do to themselves. Maybe some fool put names like that on those miserable streets to give us black folks inspiration. Or to make fun of us. Or first the one thing, then the other. Never mind. Nobody would want to hear the names I'd give them. Like Cancer and Gunshot, Weeping and Dead

Streets. Old and Broke and Jobless Avenues.

As I eased along Piety Street, the very saddest of all, I saw some boys walking past the dark buildings. One of them had a big portable radio, and the others were dancing and moving their shoulders to the music. They noticed my car going past slowly, almost silently, and the motion stopped. They didn't know my name, but they knew what I was about. On Piety and Pleasure and Abundance, you can smell cop by the time you're four.

I looked at them and knew everything but their names, and their names didn't matter. They were thieves and petty pushers, bullies and rapists and dog dumb. They were in school because of the law or dropped out in spite of it. They didn't know their fathers' names and didn't care, and their mothers counted them as a couple hundred bucks a month from the state and maybe loved them and maybe didn't. They had never had a job and nobody in his right mind would hire them or trust them or have any use for them. Not now. Not ever.

And sooner or later we'd find them one by one face down in the weeds of a vacant lot on Agriculture Street with two or three slugs driven through, or sitting propped in a storefront or doorway on Pleasure Street, eyes wide, veins hard with heroin or coke or 'lude. Nothing fancy like DMSO. Just a dirty needle one last time on the dirty evening of the last dirty day. Nothing to cry and snivel about. As well cry for rain or for love. Ninety percent of this generation was gone. You want to cry for the four- and five-year-olds with the same destiny? Be my guest. Nothing for changing the way things are like a good cry, is there?

When I paid attention again, I was on Claiborne heading back toward Uptown. I'd had myself another look at my old times, and it had set my mind on edge. Danny— Dante—Bynum had gotten out of Desire. Before he was even born. His mother had taken the one way she knew out of the hellhole and, doing it, had picked up enough velocity and money to carry her all the way to the ragged scary end of the American dream out there on the Pacific coast.

So it looked like whatever Tyrone had said the day before out at the project when he got in Danny's face had some truth to it. It didn't matter, and anyone who blamed Camille for screwing her way out of that garbage can was stone crazy. If she thought she had to shuck me to get out, how was I gonna blame her?

St. Charles Avenue was quiet and the limbs of the old oaks on either side of the esplanade broke the street lamps' glow into a pattern of moving shadows. A breeze was coming up from the river, over the levee, down into the street. My car windows were open, and I could feel it pulsing across my face even as it stirred the oak leaves and the shadows. I pulled around the corner on General Pershing Street and parked. After a moment, I got out of the car and started up to my apartment. Just as I reached the door, I realized my mind had been so far away that somebody was walking close behind without my even knowing it.

—Bang, somebody said. —You're dead.

I didn't even go for my pistol. It would have been a year and six months too late. Maxine had her own kind of smile waiting for me when I turned around.

—You hadn't ought to do that to a man, Max.

—Man hadn't ought to let me, she answered, the smile getting a little broader. With the least touch of ice in it.

—All right, I said. —Am I supposed to ask you in for a drink?

—You could ask.

—I'm asking.

—Why, thank you. I'd love to.

See, you can make a cop out of a woman, but that don't mean you've made a woman into a cop. Last night, forget it. Tonight, I thought you'd never ask.

Inside, I opened the window to the night air and cranked up some music. I started with Chopin. Romantic, sad, everything gone, strung out, chilled and impoverished by time and circumstance. Then I saw the Desire Project record and added it to the stack. Maxine had said she liked the kid.

—You want Irish, or what?

—Irish is nice. I used to drink scotch and Seven-Up.

I shuddered and poured. I didn't say anything because I wasn't looking for an argument, and I could remember what I drank when I was twenty. Rum and Coke. I shuddered again. This time for myself.

—How did it go with Tyrone? Max asked as she sat down on my sofa and hoisted one long slender leg over the other. I tried to keep my mind on her question rather than her body. It was a near thing.

—He's gonna deal before it goes to trial. Unless he wants to come out of the slam doing his imitation of the Two-Thousand-Year-Old Man.

—You were so late getting home, I thought you might have something going.

—No, I stopped by the hospital to see Camille Bynum.

—How's she handling it?

—She says all the words like she knows what they mean, I said. —But I don't think it's really hit her what's happened.

Max nodded. —A long time ago I lost a little brother. In the project. Some kind of fever or other, and a damned doctor who couldn't spell his own name. Momma didn't come back from the cemetery for a long time. She just let us take her body home.

We drank and felt that breeze, listened to old music

from the dark side of a Polish moon. Maxine slipped out of her jacket. She was wearing one of those low-cut blouses with no sleeves at all. I was thinking maybe we ought to get this drink done and her on the road. I had never gotten myself messed up with a woman at the department. It wasn't that legendary control of mine. I just hadn't seen anything like Maxine Hawkins around.

But she wasn't looking like leaving, and I wasn't feeling like shoving her out the door. Don't ask me to file a report, but I was feeling like something was missing from my life just then. Something I couldn't look up in my little phone book with the five-year calendar and invite over for a romp. Probably Camille and her sorrow, that old white Cadillac whose occupant now had a face and a name, had made me feel that way. I was wondering if I'd come as far as I liked to think—or if coming far meant anything at all. I didn't like feeling that way.

Then Danny's record started and we listened awhile in silence to his soft, anguished voice.

> . . . *Is it true, is it true, is it true what you say?*

—You think she's going to let him go?

—Nobody's asked yet. But she's not some white woman reckons she's got at least three miracles coming her way . . .

Max laughed. —Because she saved herself for her husband.

We both laughed then. —She'll let Dante go, and then try L.A. again, I guess.

Max stared at me. —Dante?

I nodded. I hadn't meant to say that, but it didn't seem like classified information, either.

—That's Danny Bynum's baptized name, I said.

She looked shocked. —Oh, boy . . . that makes me think . . . Rat, could he be . . . Nick's baby?

I was surprised how quickly she made the connection. But then no one ever said Max was slow. I shrugged and confirmed her guess. —Son of the godfather's son. Wasn't worth much to him, was it? I guess he's going on down not knowing who his daddy was.

> *... I've got to find his place, see his face,*
> *and say, Daddy, I'm just like you ...*
> *I wanna be a wise child too ...*

Maxine shook her head, looking as somber and concerned as if she was involved. —Who else knows? she asked me.

—It's not gonna be in the *Dixie Roto*, I said, drawing down on my Irish and trying to relax.

Maxine's arms and shoulders were troubling me. When she moved or lifted her glass to her lips, I could see she wasn't wearing a brassiere. Maybe I had best shove her out the door. But later, later.

We had more drinks, and I got to feeling better. Things moved along from Danny Bynum to some vintage Billy Eckstine. It happens. Outside, we heard a quiet rain begin to fall. I could see the soft blurred lights of a passing trolley, hear crackling as a wet limb brushed the wires. We found ourselves dancing without either of us suggesting, asking. Maxine leaned over and touched off the only lamp.

> *Waiter, set a table for me,*
> *A table anywhere will be all right.*
> *I just want to be alone with my memories,*
> *'Cause I'm out to forget tonight ...*

Somewhere between the third whisky and the second Eckstine side, we found ourselves on the sofa again, Max's blouse on the floor, then her skirt, my shirt and slacks. Under her blouse and skirt she'd been wearing nothing, and that nothing was enough to take your breath away. I held her as close as I could, like we were stretched through those wet singing trolley wires outside, blended together by current. She invited me in, and I went like a man going home after half a lifetime away.

> *We used to come here often*
> *To dance and share a glass of wine.*
> *Then when the lights would soften,*
> *I could feel her lips on mine...*

It was good there. It was even better in my bed where a branch the landlord always forgot to clip kept moving back and forth across the open window, splashing droplets of cool rain over our backs.

—You still on duty? I asked her after a long while.

—On or not, I always try to do my duty.

—You do, sweet woman, you do... protecting and serving.

—Are you tired? she asked me after a moment.

—Tired? Lord, how can you ask? I'm just getting up.

She laughed and pulled me over to her, kissing me like she was starved all the way down and I was the only meal in town. It seemed as if that went on for hours. Maybe it did. We couldn't get enough of each other, with the rain falling harder outside, her dark shadow against the thin light from a street lamp beyond the trees, her long silky hair down, falling over her shoulders, her skin cool to the touch, her lips moving over me everywhere, and me doing the same with her.

Somewhere during all that, I made the passage from waking to sleep. It's hard to say when, because she accompanied me into my dreams, and we kept right on keeping on with nothing changed but the illusion of duration.

Until I found myself awake with the early light, gray and faded, falling through the window, my sheets damp from that small rain that was still coming down, and the bed beside me empty and unmarked as if the dream had started when I parked my car outside the night before.

Coffee and a shower helped. Then I crawled into my wet-weather gear and started running down St. Charles as the breeze turned to a wind, leaves began to fall from the trees, and autumn came in weeping, sure enough.

Back at the apartment, I found Max had left me a note. Nothing much. Just that she had had to go home to get ready for another one of those days I put her through. She had had, I think she said, a very nice time. One thing more: she'd borrowed my Desire Project record. She wanted to tape it at her place, then she'd give it back. Fair enough. I've got lots of records. At the rate of one a night, we could have ourselves a very long, very good time.

There was a call from Denise Lemoyne when I hit the office. It was a little early for the DA's folks, but what the hell? Even lawyers have got to work sometime.

—It's about Jefferson, she told me. —He's going to have a bail hearing in about twenty minutes.

—Good, I said. —If I can catch him on the way to the pokey, maybe he'll have some stuff to tell me.

There was a long silence. —He's coming up in front of Judge Starke, Denise said at last.

—Huh? Oh, no . . . that rotten little asshole. Excuse me.

—For what? You saved me the trouble.

—You think he'll bail that shitheap?

—Nothing's slowed Starke down yet. I'm going to do

the best I can, Rat, but you know what we're up against.

—If he gives Tyrone bail, Tyrone's gonna tell me to hike. He'll worry about the charges later.

—Yep.

—Nothing we can do?

—Not a thing. In its wisdom, the System...

—Oh, baby, don't do that to me.

—That's the bad news. I've got some good.

—I can use it. Now, not later.

—CID sent over the first tape from Burnucci's TV monitor. The recording's clear as a bell.

—Probably just a lot of bullshit about zucchini and Bardolino.

—For now. But they don't have the kind of business you can put on hold, Rat. If the old man wants to stay in the hospital, sooner or later he'll have to talk to somebody. His people have to know what to do.

Denise was right. The old man had to stay in the hospital a decent time, or he'd never be able to use the heart-attack route again. But business down in the streets moved. Deals had to be made, inventory bought and moved in, orders had to be given. And Franco couldn't trust Nick. If he ever thought he could, he'd learned different with the wire fiasco at the Vegas East. Until he redeemed himself, Nick was going to be taking orders, not giving 'em. Maybe the old man'd turn up the volume on a radio and whisper under it. Maybe we'd miss it one way or another. But sooner or later, Franco Burnucci was going to talk.

Two hours later, I was standing in the Art Deco corridors of Criminal Justice with Denise. Tyrone's arraignment had gone down just the way we figured. A million worth of cocaine, a string of felony charges that damned near exhausted the criminal code—and Judge Starke put Tyrone back on the street for $100,000. Chump char ge for a big dealer.

—You know, I was telling Denise as we waited outside the clerk's office, —that little honky fucker Starke's killing black kids. They'll be dealing cut-rate tonight. Tyrone's gonna need the money for lawyers.

Denise nodded. She knew what I knew. But she and all the other good lawyers had to believe in the System. They say we don't have anything else. If they're right, we're all up Shit Creek, and the hoods have got the paddles.

Tyrone came out of the clerk's office looking like he'd just made a withdrawal at the Hibernia Bank. He was talking to his attorney and a couple of bloods in sharkskin suits who worked for him. Then he saw us.

—Well, it's the Rat...and the lady DA. Why youall picking on dis year colored boy?

—Save it for Amos and Andy, dipshit, I told him. —We got to talk.

Tyrone looked at me in mock amazement. —Me? Talk to you? Shit, Guidry, do I have to talk to that great big mean-looking nigger cop?

His lawyer looked embarrassed. I didn't blame him. The System also says you have to pay your bills if you want to keep a law office open. Guidry shook his head and looked away. Tyrone gave me this big smile with one gold tooth in it.

—Counsel says I tell you to fuck off, fool. Don't ask me the time, 'cause I won't tell.

Denise and I watched them go. The sharkskin suits were nervous. They kept looking back at me. Not Tyrone. He just kept walking on his fat little legs. He'd forgotten the Hail Mary and the Act of Contrition. If we got crossed up again, he wouldn't have time to say either one.

—This is getting to be a habit, Denise frowned.

—What?

—You and me watching the bad guys walk down this damned hallway, and out.

—Ah, sister, it's the System. We're not going to quarrel with the . . . System.

She snapped her head around, anger and humor fighting for place. —Smartass, she said, as Wes walked up to join us. He glanced down the hall in the direction we were looking.

—You guys been at bat again? Shutout?

—No. Shut up, Denise said. —I don't need it. Rat doesn't need it.

—Youall sure as hell need something.

We went over to the Two Sisters Kitchen off Claiborne and did a fine gumbo. Then fried buster crabs and hush puppies. Denise had no problem with the cuisine, and we all cursed the goddamn System and plotted against the whites.

—You reckon you could rattle Tyrone's cage once more? Wes asked. —If you caught him dirty again, even Starke . . .

—You tired of my company? I asked him. —I was lucky that first time because the little gizmo didn't reckon on one man coming through his pickets. Try it again, I wouldn't get past Abundance.

—Let's see what we get on the hospital bug, Denise suggested. —If Jefferson's one of Burnucci's people, he's wanting to know how they're going to take care of him. He's on the street, but those charges stand.

—What'll you bet he fades, I said. —Tyrone's going to Chicago or New York. Not today or tomorrow, but he's got to go.

—That's not as easy as it used to be, Wes said. —You can run, but you can't hide.

—Horseshit. You can hide, make a living, and have yourself a fine time with nice clean girls. All at the same time.

—Not forever, Denise said.

—Never mind forever. Nobody lives that long. The heat dies down, and somebody else takes your place on the list. You're wanted, but not bad wanted.

Wes shrugged. —He's got you there, Princess.

Denise looked forlorn. —Maybe I'm in the wrong business, she said softly. —Maybe I should have stuck with history.

—It's a dirty job, Wes laughed, —but...

—Let her be, man. I feel like this every fucking day about three-thirty in the morning. I wake up thinking of the ones who got away... and the other ones who died without any justice at all.

We broke it up and I went back to work. There was nothing on the street about the go at Peetie and me. Dead silence. Nothing surprising in that. It wasn't like some poor old Italian grocer out on Danneel Street getting blown away for seven dollars, a six-pack of beer, and a sack of boiled shrimp. This one was business, and people don't talk about business. Business is business.

When I got back to the office, the phone was ringing.

—Trapp here...

—I know. Miss me? Maxine asked.

—Just thinking about you, I lied politely.

—You're not going to tell, are you?

—Tell what?

—That I didn't make it this morning.

—Baby, after the way you made it last night?

Maxine laughed softly. —It was... very good. You're not ticked off about the record?

—It's yours. You can have my whole collection. Price

is the same for every one. When do you want to make your next pickup?

—Maybe soon.

—Can't be soon enough. You feeling bad?

—Just a touch hung-over . . . and wore out. I slept late . . . till a phone call woke me up. Rat, you remember Donny Jefferson?

—Small dark man. Runs a pharmacy on St. Claude Street?

—Uh-huh.

—Wait a minute. That's Tyrone's little brother. But he's all right.

—You got him. He was the one who called.

—Yeah?

—We grew up together. In the project.

—Yeah?

—It was a long time after you.

—Okay. So Donny called you.

—He told me Tyrone wants to talk.

—He's doing his own drugs. Tyrone fluffed me a couple of hours ago outside court.

—Donny told me that. He said Tyrone can't talk where anybody can see. Not even his own people.

—His own . . . well, Tyrone's got himself up a stump, don't he?

—Rat, don't do him that. He wants to come on in. He wants to roll over. But after Peetie . . .

—Shit, woman, he may have done Peetie.

—You don't believe that. Tyrone says he'll meet with you tonight.

—Piss on him. He knows where my office is.

—Rat, he'd never make it. You can't refuse. This is too big.

—Nothing is big about Tyrone but his mouth and his ass.

—Well, let me get done so I can tell Donny I tried. Desire, Building Nineteen, apartment Two-A. Any time after eleven, but nobody else comes.

—Okay, you've told me.

—You want me to come along? I know that place. He'd never know I was there.

—Forget it. I don't know I'm going. I got a few other ribs cooking just now.

—Oh? Tell me . . .

—Nothing worth the time, girl. Get yourself together and come on in. I'll cover for this morning.

Max thanked me and hung up. I thought about it all for a while. We didn't have anything on Donny Jefferson. So far as I knew, he was clean. He and Tyrone had gone to pharmacy school about the same time, and they'd run the little drugstore together till Tyrone got his license lifted. Seems he was moving about twenty to thirty times as much controlled substance as the big chain drugstores in town. Drug companies didn't give a shit, but the chain stores did, so they yelled for the feds to wake up from beside their taping machines, and Tyrone did close to two years when it had all settled.

Now Donny was calling Max, telling her about how I was supposed to meet Tyrone. I wanted to go, no doubt about that.

Looking at the up side, it might be straight. Tyrone was looking at eight to fifteen for all that dope he'd scattered over Claiborne Avenue even if his lawyer had a lock on the court. But if he could make the Burnuccis for us, the state and the feds would walk him in a Shreveport second, as Wes says. He'd have to watch himself after that, but he'd have his money and his ass, and the world opens out if you've got the bucks.

Looking at the down side, maybe Tyrone was just getting petty. Maybe he reckoned he'd likely have to do his time sooner or later and just wanted the pure pleasure of putting out a couple of cigars in my eyes before he pounded me a new pair in the back of my head. But that didn't sound like Tyrone. Worst I knew about him, Tyrone was a businessman. If he could have made more money flogging prayerbooks around the project, he'd have put on a bishop's hat and learned himself some Latin.

As I went through it all in my mind, I realized I'd already decided. I was going. No way I wasn't going. If I didn't go, and it turned out later Tyrone had wanted to take a leak on the Burnuccis, I'd never get over it.

Anyhow, I know what I'm doing, and I'm lucky. Even if it was a setup, I had a better chance of walking away than Tyrone did. Yes, love, I was going, all right. But I was going my way. And my way is something to behold.

CHAPTER
9

I checked out with the watch and called Wes Colvin.

—You need a story, or are you just killing time till you see Denise tonight?

—Denise has a status conference at five. She said not to wait around.

—Reckon she'd let you come out and play with me tonight?

—Not if she knew about it.

We met at my place about nine. Wes was curious, and I filled him in. He didn't like my idea much.

—Come on, Rat. Tell Mauvais.

—I wouldn't tell that old bastard his own name.

—You need some backup, and I sure as hell ain't it.

—Don't low-rate yourself. After all, you created me, remember? I got a lot of faith in you.

—Then you're not fit for duty. Where's the whisky?

He knew where the whisky was. He poured us a couple and watched while I was getting myself ready for our little mixer out at Desire.

—Why don't you give up this Super Cop thing and get serious about politics?

—It's crossed my mind now and again. I got your vote for City Council?

—You got my vote for anything up to Prince of Darkness, but you got to be alive to serve.

—I'll see to politics later, I told him. —Right now I want to hang it in Burnucci.

Wes rolled his eyes. —You're gonna stop the dope trade single-handed.

—Nope. Just carve on Burnucci.

—Which Burnucci? Wes asked slyly.

—Hah.

I had pulled my old army trunk from the closet and was laying out my play toys as we talked. I found the MAC-10 and the silencer that fit it and five or six clips of 9mm ammo. Wes stared at it.

—Remember it? I asked him.

His eyes widened. He remembered it all right. A while back, we'd waded through some tough times together, when a crazy had used the same gun to clean out a Quarter bar.

—Lester's...?

—Ah, I said, —you sentimental thing.

—How the hell did you get it?

—Come on. The NOPD property office is looser than a gill net. One day it was in there, the next day it was gone. I got me a new barrel for it. No ballistics at all.

I pulled out a couple of concussion grenades and one fragmentation and laid them on the bed. I still had this black coverall with pockets all over it, and a flak jacket and body armor from my free-lancing in Germany. There was a Walther PPK with a silencer, and six or eight mini-claymores.

If Tyrone's folks had in mind to do me, best they had

allies in the East zone. I hung my old stiletto around my neck on a lanyard. Wes frowned.

—That thing looks sharp and clean.

—Never a week goes by, I told him.

—What have you got for me? he asked.

I picked up the Uzi that lay wrapped in oil paper down at the bottom of the trunk along with half a dozen more clips of 9mm. He held it, looked it over, and smiled with relief.

—I thought you were going to hand me a police whistle.

We laughed and walked back to the parlor for some more hooch. Wes seemed surprised.

—You reckon it's smart to drink if we're gonna...

—I never worked wet trade in Germany unless I was stoned to the gills, I told him. —Anyhow, you're just gonna drive. You're gonna park on Treasure Street right across from Building Nineteen at the project. You're gonna lock your doors and stay low. If anybody comes up, you're gonna stick that Uzi in his face. If he tries the door, you're gonna blow his head off. Otherwise, just wait till you see me.

—I'm gonna drive you to Tyrone's place?

—No way. I'm coming in the back. If Tyrone's got folks watching, they're all gonna be watching you.

Wes nodded, stared down into his liquor. —Fucking bait. So I'm gonna have the meanest niggers in Desire, armed to the teeth, watching my car.

Wes is not your basic racist. He just picks his blacks like a tasteful man would. Far as that goes, I guess we're both racists. Piss on the races. We do dearly love each other.

—You want to use some burnt cork, old son?

—Hell, they won't care what color I am. Will they?

—Truth to tell, you're probably right. But if old Ty is playing me straight, there won't be anybody hassling you except maybe the ones who strip cars.

—What about them? Can I off me a couple?

—I wouldn't do that. But you see my car's able to run. If they want the side mirrors, no sweat. We all got to eat. If they go for the tires or the engine, fire a burst down at the pavement.

—Mighty white of you, he said as we headed for the door.

It was a dark night, no moon, clouds heavy and low. There was a front coming through and the autumn wind was whipping trees and shrubs around as Wes dropped me off in an empty lot near the project. When I looked back, I saw his pale face framed in the driver's window and wondered how come a man with a job and a lovely woman like Denise would get himself involved in this kind of offbeat stuff. I probably knew the answer as well as Wes did. Every so often we need the shit scared out of us. It makes life better. The proper way to get the shit scared out of us is doing something that needs doing. With friends. After a few seconds, the car drifted away.

I moved through the tall unmown grass and weeds, across a stinking little gulley filled with garbage and trash that caught and held the rain, and through a rusty broken fence on the edge of the Desire property. A stark gray building defaced with spray-paint signs loomed up in front of me. SYRIS LOVE MOLISSA, I found out, and VICTER IS A FRUT AN A PUNK. I eased up to the edge of the building, stepping over a trashed bike frame.

If my calculating was right, Building Nineteen would be right across the court at a forty-five-degree angle. But I was going around the long way. The building I was leaning up against was the only one that had a clear view of Nineteen and Abundance Street, too. If Tyrone was straight, I could walk right across the muddy court covered with broken bottles and trash paper and into Nineteen—if I moved fast and none of the bloods was roving. If it was a setup, there'd be people upstairs in this building. I decided to check out the roof.

Inside, one sixty-watt bulb dangled from a wire down at the end of the first-floor hall. I was surprised. It must have got put in that day. No lightbulb owned by the city lasted more than a few hours.

As I moved upstairs, a door opened on a guard chain. An old lady looked out, frowning, fearful.

—Go on back in, Auntie, I told her as she stared at my MAC-10. —Nothing's happening. You ain't seen nothing.

The door slammed shut, and I headed for the stairs that would take me to the roof. As I made a corner, I saw a knot of boys standing at the far end of the hall passing a joint back and forth between 'em. The biggest one must have stood six-four or -five. He looked up and started walking down the corridor toward me. Just what I hadn't wanted to happen.

—Say, Dude . . . whatall you got there? he asked, just like we were old buddies. The rest of 'em closed in behind, and I had wall-to-wall outlaws coming to check me out.

—I got your balls in my pocket and your dick in my hand, I told him. —Get lost, or I'll lose you.

—Strong, man, strong. Do I know you? Like you so bad . . .

He was wearing a stocking cap with a big cotton bunnytail on top, and a black nylon windbreaker. He had a bad complexion and his eyes looked like dirty snowballs. He had his hand behind him like I had mine behind me. Unless police intelligence was all fucked up, I had a better hand. But I give him this. He did move fast. He came up from behind with a little piss-ant Hi Standard .22 like they made back in the fifties. He got off one shot that hit my jacket low on the left and made racket enough to warn Tyrone, the quick and the dead.

—*Chuf chuf chuf*, my MAC-10 whispered, and the ceiling of the hallway started to cave in. My bloods got covered with plaster, filled with bone-deep panic. Big Boy up front dropped his .22 and disappeared in the plaster dust. In two seconds, I had me a wrecked hallway all to myself.

The roof was clear, but I wondered if it had been before Big Boy and his folks had gone to jiving with me. Maybe I'd find out.

Back outside, I skirted behind two other buildings, and found myself an open window in the rear of Building Nineteen. This part was tricky. People in Desire own half the guns in New Orleans, and they got every reason in the world to cut loose at anything that pokes its head through their window. Whatever the hell it is, it's not gonna be the Welcome Wagon.

I levered myself up on the windowsill and looked in, ready to drop back and roll if the folks inside happened to be doing their neighborhood watch. But the room was empty. It had a bed and a bureau in it, and I could see the shaky blue reflection of a TV hitting the open door from the far room. Being lucky is better than being good, I thought, as I climbed into the room and moved across it. If there was gonna be trouble, at least I'd be able to meet it standing up with my big MAC out front.

No trouble at all. In the parlor a woman and three or four kids huddled around her like kittens had fallen asleep in front of the TV. Yeah, well, Johnny Carson has the same effect on half the insomniacs in America.

I eased out into the hall and closed the door behind me. Theeeeeere goes Rat, I thought. And the kids never even got to see me.

At the foot of the stairs, I paused, checking out my

stuff. If Tyrone was trying to out-think me, he'd drawn himself a really tight perimeter. His boys would have cleared out all the occupied apartments on the second floor so nobody would know—and so I'd have no place to back up to. But I didn't believe that. If you do things right, you don't leave the ground floor full of women and kids sleeping in front of the TV.

Time to go on up and shake Tyrone out. I only hoped he was going to be worth the trouble. I'm not twenty-three or even thirty anymore. I don't need all this cowboy crap.

Apartment Two-A was down on the left next to a big open window at the end of the corridor. I moved down, watching the other doors, looking back every other second. It must have looked like a rerun of *Combat* on the tube. Then I was as far as I could go. Two-A. Fish or cut bait. In or out. What was it Wes always said? Oh, yeah: no guts, no glory.

I kicked in the door and spun through, landing on my belly with the big MAC sniffing the shadows around the edge of the room. There was one dim lamp on over by the sofa that Tyrone was sitting on with a big ugly pistol in his hands. Right behind him on the wall was a dumb-looking painting of Jesus suffering the little children.

Tyrone? Pistol? I almost let him have it, but the barrel of his gun was pointing at the floor like it had melted in the heat of the stuffy room. I had time to look my man over.

—Put it down, Tyrone. You don't need it. Daddy's gonna take you on home.

See, my attention wasn't altogether on Tyrone. I had that busted door at my back, and doors on my right and left there in the room that led somewhere. I got up and put my back against some kind of armoire in the corner.

If somebody out in the hall went to stitching .44 Magnum slugs through those project walls, even my jacket wasn't gonna help.

—Tyrone, drop the fucking piece and get on your feet.

Up in the corner, feeling about as snug as I could, I had time to look over at Tyrone and study him. For just a second, it looked like he was staring back at me. Then I saw blood running down the front of his designer sweatshirt. Three patches right over left center. Two more than suicide said.

I made a careful move toward him and right then the lamp behind the sofa went out. I heard a door open, and all hell broke loose. There were four or five silenced shots as fast as I could count 'em. Oh, shit, I remember thinking. It wasn't Tyrone setting me up. It was somebody using him to...

I had dropped to the floor when that light cut off, and rolled. Now I was on my back like an upended turtle. Fuck it. I sprayed Big MAC all over the goddamned place like it was a garden hose. *Chuf chuf chuf chuf chuf.* No favorites. Every wall, the ceiling, both doors and the hallway outside got their fair share of slugs.

I heard a soft distant sigh like somebody finishing love, then everything got quiet. Not that it had been loud. Whoever's pistol and my submachine gun both spoke real low. People in the apartment across the hall may not have heard a sound. Even if they had, they weren't coming out to look around.

After a few minutes, I found a light switch on the wall. Tyrone was right where he'd been before, only slumped over to one side. Seems my garden-hose move had put a couple of 9mms into him. But Tyrone didn't give a shit. He was above or beneath it all, or turned off, or whatever we are when our neighbors get done kicking shit out of us here on earth.

One of the doors was ajar now, and I stormed on into the kitchen, reckoning to find nothing at all. Not quite. There were a few drops of blood on the floor, and a rill of it on a table. Outside, there was a set of wooden stairs leading down to the ground. The back screen door was still swaying from somebody's hand or the autumn wind. Out beyond the building, it was black as the devil's armpit. I pulled back, just in case somebody had in mind to give me one more go when I stuck my head out with the kitchen light behind me.

I went back into the parlor and looked down at old Tyrone. So somebody had found out after all that Tyrone wanted to talk to me. How you gonna keep a secret in the project? Everybody who might give a shit knew I was about and around. I closed Tyrone's eyes, wondering if he'd had a chance to get off that last Hail Mary, wondering if it mattered or not.

After I used my car radio and called for a Homicide team to come see to Tyrone, Wes drove us Uptown to his place. Wes had the notion that if they'd waited around after chopping down Tyrone to get me, I had to be a misery to somebody. It seemed likely whoever had tried might give it one more once, and he judged maybe his apartment was safer than mine.

We poured drinks before anything else. Even before Wes saw that I was bleeding on his favorite big wing chair. Seems all that fancy shooting hadn't gone altogether to waste. I had a nice crease across the point of my left shoulder. It was just beginning to hurt. Wes poured some whisky on it.

—Oh, shit . . .

—Want me to set a match to it?

—You fucking Ku-Kluxer. You can't do that shit to a cop.

—Raiding Desire at night with a machine gun. Some cop.

—Christ, you know it ain't easy. You know how hard it can be...

I filled him in on the details, him nodding and drinking. But I went too far. When I told him about hitting Tyrone when I was break dancing on my back with Big MAC talking, he laughed.

—Good God, you shot...a dead man?

It was a private joke, but it made me laugh till the tears came to my eyes. Or maybe the shoulder was hurting more than I wanted to let on.

—So you reckon it was the Burnuccis?

—I bet Nick spent the evening with his old daddy, and they had a nurse come in every ten minutes or so just to prove it up.

—But why go for you? They don't have enough trouble without killing a cop?

—What am I supposed to tell you? Killing Peetie was a necessity. Peetie was gonna make the old man. And maybe they worried about Tyrone talking.

—Okay. But why try for you? Maybe the Burnuccis just don't want you on their case?

—They'll sure as hell have to kill me to get me off it, I told Wes.

I'd gone after the old man out of something like professional pride. He'd thought he could wing a couple of hits right past me. But now I had a personal stake in it. It was that damned white Cadillac that kept me going. I wanted Nick Burnucci to fall, and I wanted him to fall because *I* did it to him. And I wanted him to know why.

—Maybe they've got the rest of the department in their pocket, I added. —Maybe they bought Mauvais back when I was a kid.

But Wes wasn't paying any attention. He was behind

his portable computer, logging in, typing as fast as he could. He had a mean grin on his face.

—I'll have this in to the paper and set up before the poor bastards they sent out to cover your report can even find the right building.

By then, I had a piece of gauze and some tape over the shoulder, my second drink under my belt, and all my traps—guns, knives, and whatnot—ready to go.

Wes looked up from that hot computer of his. —Where do you think you're going?

—The night is young. I got me a druggist I need to talk to.

—Pain pills? No problem. I got a cabinet full of stuff that would knock out an elephant. You ever have a Percodan in your martini?

—Ha. You must have made a friend out of Tyndall.

—That creep? Naw. I got my own connections. What do you need with a druggist?

—Not any old druggist. Donny Jefferson, Tyrone's brother. The rat's ass sonofabitch set me up.

—Huh?

—He told Maxine that Tyrone wanted to see me.

—Reckon he had a gun in his ear?

—I don't give a fuck. He's gonna have my foot up his ass when I find him.

—Come back afterward, Wes said, looking serious. —You can have the couch. I don't want to think of you sleeping in that apartment by yourself.

I popped him on the shoulder on my way out. —You got it. Just for the sake of your nerves.

—Anyhow, he called after me, —if it happens here, I got a beat on the story.

St. Claude Street doesn't look like much in broad daylight. It's a wide urban street with old buildings and rundown businesses, vacant lots, and little two-bit shops. Deep night is a little kinder to it. Then it looks like something the Ashcan School might have painted. Pools of cold light from streetlamps, washes of shadow, slivers of quartz in broken curbstones twinkling like fractured stars in the street, night lamps aching behind dirty windows. Painted signs so faded you can't even make out what it is the people inside are selling. If they're still selling anything at all. If they're even still alive in there.

Jefferson's Pharmacy stood out because the sidewalk in front was swept, the signs legible, and the windows clean enough to see that the displays inside were of products still being manufactured. You couldn't always count on that along St. Claude. There was a single light burning back over the pharmacist's dark wood counter, and the place looked like someone had locked up and walked out in 1937.

As I remembered, the Jefferson brothers had lived above the store when Donny and Tyrone ran it. Now that Donny had taken over the place by himself, I expected he still did.

I pushed the bell and stayed on it. After a little, a woman with her hair up in curlers leaned out an upstairs window.

—What you want, man? The store's closed. Get on away from here.

I held my badge up in my left hand so that some of that cold light glanced off it. The other hand was inside my coveralls, kind of resting on my .357. I didn't know who was up there, or just what they might have in mind. If anything scarier than that woman's head poked out the window, I wasn't gonna be standing there with my thumb up my ass.

—Ralph Trapp, New Orleans Police. I want Donny Jefferson. Down here. At the door. Hands out in front. He knows the routine.

—Oh, sweet Jesus. Donny...old man...

She was back inside then, calling out toward the back of the place. It sounded all right. If Donny tried vanishing this time of night, I'd have him in an hour. Every place he knew, I knew. And people there didn't owe him anything but a shot of whisky for a dollar and a half. Everybody owes me—or is fixing to.

Another light came on downstairs, and, sure enough, here came Donny, bald, except for a nice little gray fringe over his ears and around behind, wearing metal-rimmed glasses, eyes the size of billiard balls, hands out in front of him like he was expecting me to hand him a mess of fish. He showed me the keys and fumbled with the door until it came open. When it did, he was already talking.

—It's not me, officer. You got to be looking for my brother. See, he...

I pushed him back inside. —I already found Tyrone, I told him. —What I want to know is what he told you to pass on to me.

We went to the back, and Donny poured himself a shot of Wild Turkey. He had to use both hands to steady it. He hadn't seen Tyrone since last Easter. And that was all right. It had almost cost Donny his pharmacist's license when Tyrone lost his.

I kept my eyes tight on him. He started to sit down on a tall stool. I pulled it away and sat on it myself. His lips were trembling, and it occurred to me I'd been wrong earlier. He was Tyrone's older brother, and, yes, he would have lost his license before you could spit if he hadn't been clean and able to prove it. Too many black pharmacists in Orleans Parish. The licensing board wouldn't mind cutting back.

In the hallway behind where we were standing, I could see the woman with her hair in some kind of pink plastic curlers, two or three kids behind and beside her watching me like I was the boogie man. I was. I wanted them to know that. It's no use lying to the boogie man. He knows your every thought. You got to come clean, or he'll take you away. Everybody knows that.

Ten minutes in, I was convinced Donny didn't know anything. Maxine had told me she talked to Donny Jefferson. That was bullshit. He didn't know her, or if he ever had, he couldn't remember. He didn't know much more about Tyrone. Only that he was still doing what he'd lost his license and some free time for doing before. And I believed every word Donny Jefferson said. Nobody bullshits to me that good for that long. That made my lady Maxine a lying bitch who had tried to tie me to the rails right when the Express was coming through. I took a deep breath and nodded.

—All right.

He stared back at me. —What's . . . all right?

—All right is, I'm not gonna bust your black ass 'cause you tried to set me up. At least not now.

He started in to tell me the whole thing all over again about how his brother was a shiftless lowlife nigger nobody could trust. I thought how weird it was that he and I and most all of us, when we're pushed a little, use the same language on one another that the Man used to use on us. What the hell? Who remembers the Swahili translation?

—Stop it, I told him.

—What?

—Never mind low-rating Tyrone.

—But he's a . . .

—Not anymore. He's nothing. Somebody done him at the project.

Donny stared up at me like he didn't understand. He understood all right. He'd been waiting to hear it since we were all in school together, maybe picturing in his mind how the news would come and how he'd feel. Now it had come on him in the middle of the night after he'd just been scared loose from sleep and jerked around by a big cop he didn't even recognize. His expression never changed. If he hadn't been standing under that night-light, I couldn't have even seen the tears running down his cheeks.

—Oh, my Christ, the woman whispered.

—Whatsa matter, Momma? one of the kids asked.

—Go upstairs, honey. Take the babies.

—Something bad gonna happen, Momma?

—No, baby. Go on, now.

Donny frowned at me then, moved closer, his eyes digging into mine.

—Did you do Ty? Was it you?

—No.

—Then . . . ?

—He was gone when I got to him. Then somebody tried me.

—I told him, the woman said. —Donny, didn't I tell him about that place?

—Yeah, you told him.

—God, to die in Desire, she groaned.

—It's not much good anywhere, I said, and walked out past the old dark wooden shelves heavy with Dr. Tichnor's Antiseptic and Royal Crown Hairdressing and Garrett's Snuff. I pulled the door closed behind me and started for the car. I had just reached it and was fumbling for my keys when I heard Donny Jefferson give out a cry that sounded like a man dying. Of a wound he'd been expecting all his life.

CHAPTER
10

I got on the horn and somebody in Operations woke up enough to shake out Maxine Hawkins's personnel jacket. Her home address was on the river side of St. Charles, the black end of Hillary Street. Small houses with chain-link fences, a few palmettos, and elephant ears in the yard. Mostly working-class people who'd had the sense and discipline to buy a little place when one of those shotguns sold for six or seven thousand dollars. Now they were sitting on property worth at least ten times as much. A lot of them would've taken the money and run—except there's still neighborhoods in New Orleans. Five generations of a family may live and die in a six-block area. If that's where you've always been, where would you go? Even with a grocery bag full of money?

When I got somebody to come to the door, it was like playing the tune I'd played at Donny Jefferson's all over again. I wasn't bringing anybody good news that night.

Jade Hawkins was a good-looking woman of about fifty. Right at first, she wasn't going to talk at all.

—Max doesn't live here, does she?

—She did. This is her home whenever she wants it. She's not in trouble, is she?

—Do you know who I am, Mrs. Hawkins?

She knew my name, knew that Maxine worked for me. She knew I could fire her or make it all right. After a little more fencing, it came out the way I figured. Maxine had never lived in the house on Hillary. She'd moved her mother out of Desire and into it a year and a half after starting on the force. She'd told her mother she could afford it, she was making good money. But she wanted a place of her own. Max had an apartment in River Tower, a new complex that overlooks the Mississippi near Audubon Park.

Jade Hawkins looked something past worried. She had to know it took more than a cop's salary to move her to Hillary Street—and hold down a place in River Tower. I knew that tight intense hopeless look on her face. She'd brought it with her from Desire. Call it fear of falling.

—You're not gonna mess her up, are you?

—I'll see what I can do, I told her, and got back out to the street as fast as I could.

Max Hawkins was already messed up. Just then, I was wondering how bad. She'd bought the house her mother was in after the prices had gone all the way up. She was living at an address other than her personnel file reported—and the rents at River Tower started at a couple grand a month.

River Tower loomed out of the trees and shadows like a rocket over at the Cape. Up its round side, you could see the exposed elevator shafts gleaming, set off by the hallway glow behind. Here and there, people who could pay two or three thousand a month for a roof over their heads still had their lights on. It was nice to know some of the bastards had to stay up all night to figure their next move.

I parked and sat thinking. Wes would have filed his story on Tyrone by now, and the early edition was probably on the street. I wondered if Maxine had seen it and already knew she'd run out of luck, that I'd gone through her story and was on my way. Lord, I remembered the cool autumn air playing across us in my bed. Easing me in, setting me up. I'd been played and laid before, but not like that. I had never looked to get my ass blown off because I was screwing when I should have been working. A Russian woman had tried something like it in Berlin. I'd thrown her out a third-story window. Maxine lived on the fifteenth floor. Five times worse.

I thought about calling in and getting a backup, but I passed. I like to do my own work. I don't want 'em watching, and I don't want 'em fucking me up. If Maxine's people were up there, I'd just have to manage it myself. It's brains and hardware, not how many people you go in with.

The security guard inside the door was trouble. Not a lot, but trouble. He took one look at my MAC-10 and couldn't seem to focus on the badge. He kept telling me he was going to have to get authority. Then he started in on this thing about calling Miss Hawkins and telling her I was on the way up.

—Motherfucker, do I look like I want to be announced?

—It could mean my job. I got no authority to let you...

—What if I shoot your leg off? Would that make it all right?

He decided he didn't really give a shit about the job when it came down to that. As I moved off toward one of the fancy elevators, I looked back.

—If you touch that phone board, I'm gonna come back, jerk your ass off, and pull it down over your head like a toilet seat, hear?

He heard, and he obeyed. All that is required for effective police communication is a clearly declared purpose forcefully expressed. You like that? I heard it at some FBI seminar I went to.

The elevator was really nice. Its glass shaft looked east, away from the river. As I rode up high over the trees and the quiet streets and the dark houses, I could see the sky going from black to deep blue to gray. I noticed that tall clouds had drifted in from the Gulf during the night. What they call an overrun, where that warm air comes back over cool air below. Before I reached the fifteenth floor, it began to rain softly, the drops hitting against the glass of the elevator, running down, blowing away in the wind like the rain off a jet's window when you're taking off into a storm.

The corridor was bright as noon, silent, empty. I didn't like it even though I knew it was supposed to be that way. I got my bearings and started moving down toward 1533. She'd be sleeping now—or not. Just depending on what she knew and what she—and her people—meant to do about it. If she was alone, I wondered if she'd try to make her best deal. The kind she could make so well if she just shrugged those dark golden shoulders and let her gown fall to the floor. I stopped and shook my head. I was thinking like a man who wanted to die sometime in the next five minutes or so. If you mix up killing and fucking, you better stay home with the TV.

The door of 1533 was a warm brown with one of those peepholes in the middle. I decided I didn't want to be peeped. As I stood wondering just how hard to go in, I could hear a phone buzzing softly inside. That sonofa-bitch downstairs was gonna hurt when I got done. I can lift a security guard's weapons permit easier than I can fix a parking ticket in the Quarter.

I was about to kick the door down for openers when it came to me that I was hearing that phone mighty clear—

and that no one was answering it. I squinted at the door before I kicked. It wasn't closed all the way. Like somebody had pushed it to and paid no mind if the lock snapped or not. Good.

I got down low and pushed it open with the silencer of the MAC-10. A long shaft of bright light from the hall behind me cut through the darkness inside, and I moved after it ready to do my garden-hose bit again if things went bad.

The room had one low lamp burning on a table next to a floor-to-ceiling sliding-glass door that led out to a balcony on the far side. The phone was on that table, still chuckling away in a genteel fashion. I stood up and let the hall door close behind me just the way it had been before. If leaving in a hurry got to be the thing, I didn't want to fight a dry lock.

It was some apartment. If you didn't know better, you'd say a time machine had sent you back to the late twenties or the thirties. Somebody with a lot of taste and more money had brought Art Deco to life again. Lucite and chrome, rich lacquer and marble were everywhere. There was a big canvas of the Chrysler Building on one wall, painted from a perspective that made it look like a spaceship. Sofas, chairs, even a long table against the wall— all done in pastel plastics. The single lamp burning had an Oriental lacquer base and a brushed-aluminum shade. The sliding-glass doors had been frosted lightly with a design of flowers, tropical plants, stylized birds—and the dancing nude figure of a woman whose smiling face surrounded with piled hair looked exactly like Maxine.

I checked out the kitchen, the balcony. Nothing. By then the phone had stopped ringing, and I could hear music in the distance, hardly louder than the background noise in my ears. I had only the bedroom left to go through, and I was thinking that, after all, Max was a smart girl.

By now, she was probably in Houston or Atlanta, heading for a nice safe place where men of eminence keep folks who do them services.

The bedroom door was open a crack, and I looked in. The bed was king-sized with ornamental pillars and a canopy that looked like one of those competition parachutes. The room seemed to glow with a low level of light that came from the bathroom. She's taking a shower, I thought. Maybe I ought to let her finish and get some clothes on. There I was, at it again. Brain turned to Pussy-Whip.

But there was no sound of water, nothing that said something human was going on in there. Only that soft music that sounded so distant I could almost believe it was playing in my head. Then I could make out a few words.

Wise child . . . wise child . . .

Danny Bynum's record. The one Maxine had walked away with. Maybe she thought it belonged to her now. Inheritance from a sucker.

That pushed me through the door to the bedroom. The corners of the room were dark and empty, the furniture crouched around the walls concealed no one. I glanced at a pile of dark clothes on the scarlet-and-beige-satin bedcover and then moved toward that light in the bathroom like a cautious moth. When I shoved open the door with my piece, I pulled up short.

Once the bathroom must have been a joy of clear plastic, long mirrors, tan gold-veined marble tub and lavatory, white high-pile rug on the floor, filled with hard golden light. Now it looked like the workroom in a butcher shop.

The bright mirrors ran with blood, and it glistened on the marble of the lavatory. The rug's soft fibers were clotted with it, and there were long crimson smudges and handprints on the transparent shower stall.

That was it. No body, no clothing, nothing else. Wait. One thing more. A long-barreled .38 revolver with a silencer attached lying in one of those patches on the rug. The grip was dark and sticky, and the cylinder was empty. I squatted there for what seemed a long time, poking the revolver with my piece, thinking Maxine might be a long way past messed up by now. In the Wop league, they play hardball, and if they catch you off base they kill you. Max had told them she could deliver me on a platter, but somehow I'd slipped off and landed on my feet. That's a strike. You don't get three. Maybe you don't even get two.

When I walked back into the dark bedroom, I couldn't see for a moment. Danny's record was starting to play from the top again. I was about to sit down on the edge of the bed when I heard that soft sigh I remembered hearing after the shooting at Desire. I was against the wall, tight as a guy wire, the long dark barrel of the big MAC pointing this way and that. Then the crumpled clothes on the bed seemed to shiver, and I realized Maxine was at home after all.

The bedcover was just beige. The scarlet was Max's blood—the little she must have had left when she staggered out of the bathroom and fell across her elegant expensive bed. She was dressed in a black jumpsuit, and the stitching of holes across her back gleamed wetly under the subdued light.

Pity me, can't you see that I'll never be free . . .

She was drawn up into a fetal knot that had made me think she was old clothes lying on the bed. It passed through my mind again that I was getting too old for this crap. If she'd had the .38 on the bed with her, she might have gone on and finished the job she'd messed up at Desire. I tried to turn her on her back so that I could cut away the bloody jumpsuit with my stiletto.

—No, she moaned. —No...

—Keep quiet, I told her. —You're fucked up real bad.

She seemed to come to herself then, and she recognized me.

—Oh, God, she said. —You're already here. You're that fast. Jesus, I thought you were...over the hill.

—Yeah, well, they got a nigger graveyard down in the Ninth Ward. It's full of dudes that had that thought.

I was just bullshitting her along, trying to keep her conscious, not let her drift any farther into shock than she already was. I had her jumpsuit unzipped by then, and when I saw what my shots had done to her, it took all I could do not to turn away or scream or beat my head against the Lucite bedpost.

That body I'd kissed and caressed had three 9mm wounds from the lowest left rib at an angle down to the right hip. The holes across her belly were open and dark, rimmed with clotted blood. Two of the slugs had passed clean through her, carrying some of that sweet flesh away with them, and I could tell from the entry and exit positions that her right kidney had to be gone.

I checked for other wounds. There weren't any, but I suspected it didn't matter. I wanted to close my eyes, say to myself, You didn't do this. That wasn't your gun. Some animal in the project did this to her. Then I was telling myself, She didn't do it. I know how it looks, but she didn't try to waste you out at Desire. This is a nice girl who maybe got on the tab with some scumbag, but...

Just then the phone started chirping again. I reached for it as Maxine's hand fell strengthlessly away from the line.

—Maxine? Momma. I been calling. That cop, that Trapp

you work for. He was here, honey. You better give him what he wants, baby. He can hurt you, you know...?

I let the phone drop back on the cradle and broke the connection. Then I dialed Police Emergency. When I had an ambulance and a Homicide team on the way, I called downstairs.

—Lobby...

—Yeah, lobby. I got cops and corpsmen on the way. You get one of those elevators stopped and ready for 'em, hear?

—Is there an emergency? I have to call...

—There's gonna be an emergency if you even look at the phone board after I hang up. This is police business. You got that down?

—Yes, sir. I understand.

—How are you fixed for first-aid kits down there?

—Sorry, there's nothing.

—Then you do what I told you. Get those corpsmen up to 1533 as fast as your dumb white ass can move.

—Rat...

—Yeah, Max.

—Am I gonna...die?

—I don't know. You're hurt bad.

—And if I make it...

—You won't be making it on the street for a long, long time.

She nodded and tried to reach for a glass of water on her night table. I put her hand back down.

—You don't want to drink nothing.

—Shit, why not? I can see it in your eyes...gimme the water.

I let her have a sip, thinking how good it had been between us for a little while, how good it could have been for a long, long time. Once, years ago, I had lost me a partner in a two-bit 7-Eleven robbery. The old man was four months from retirement, and he bled to death in my arms. Drinking a Coke. With some rum in it. Right off the store shelf. How did it feel? Just like sitting beside Max. The only difference was, Francis Murray had never tried to kill me.

—Why? I asked her as I took away the water and set her head back down on a satin pillow.

—Like your lady, Camille Bynum. I wanted out of that garbage can we grew up in. Nobody goes for free. Ask her.

—So you started moonlighting for Burnucci?

—It came to that, she said softly. —I didn't want to sell myself...

—So you were Burnucci's ear in the department. You kept him up on police business.

—Not...everything. I didn't know Vegas East was wired...when the old man met Peetie.

—So your fuck-up got him indicted.

—I...had to take care of that.

I stared down at her. —Shit, it was you hit Peetie?

—I had to...make it up to them. God, I hated you. I...wanted you...

—Oh...?

—...dead.

—Ah...So that's why it didn't happen with us...for so long. Not till they told you to screw me.

—I've...had it worse.

—I never had it better...except...

—You got too long...a memory, Trapp.

—I'm working on it. Pretty soon I'll be able to forget in twenty minutes.

—Not me, you won't.

—No, I said, then remembered I was working. —Why Tyrone?

—Why not? You got to kill the worm to bait the hook, don't you...?

I couldn't figure it. Revenge, because I set the old man up for a retirement cell at Angola penitentiary? Hell, Burnucci could manage that anytime. Then Max answered my silent question.

—... 'Cause you just know too much, honey.

I still missed it. I was going to go on missing it for a while. I thought she meant I was the witness that could send Burnucci away.

—You know ... everything ...

The hell I did. She coughed then. A rill of blood bubbled out at the corner of her mouth and ran down her cheek as if a fountain had broken loose inside. For a moment, I thought she was going right then.

I got up and headed for the bathroom. Maybe I could find some bandages, some gauze. I had opened the medicine cabinet before I pulled myself together: you shot her. Because she shot Tyrone and tried to take you out, too. If she wasn't a woman with chocolate skin and coffee eyes, you'd sit on the edge of the bed grinning, letting her bleed to death.

My mind came back, and I realized that I was staring at a bottle labeled dimethyl sulfoxide. DMSO? And beside it on the shelf was a jar of Max Factor stage makeup. Then it hit me. Sweet Lord Jesus, she'd done Danny Bynum, too. But why?

I swept the cosmetic jar and the DMSO into one of the pockets of my coveralls, found a roll of bandages, and started back to her.

—What about Danny Bynum? I asked her. —You salted his makeup with dope and DMSO, didn't you. Why? Why would Burnucci want a kid with a rock band offed?

But Max wasn't talking anymore. She had passed out.

I hardly heard the medical people and a couple of street cops when they rolled in. One of the cops threw down on me when he saw me in my Captain Rat coveralls. I eased out my badge and explained what had gone down as the medical team started working on Maxine.

I was going out the door behind the gurney when the cop who had drawn on me called my name. I could see he wanted to win back a point or two. In one hand, he was holding an old Winchester sporting model .30–.30 with a scope as big around as a coffee can. In the other, a pile of spent brass. He'd found them in a closet.

I took the rifle and opened the chamber. The smell of powder was still there. Then I took the shell casings and studied them. In my mind, I counted the rounds that had come out of the sun a little after dawn in Baton Rouge. They were all there.

—Captain . . . ?

—Tag it, I said, tossing the piece back to him as if I'd just inspected it. He caught it the same way. —Tag it and the cartridges. Make sure you don't lose any. Tell Ballistics to check it against the Peetie Postum slugs.

—Yes, sir.

—One other thing. This is the key to my apartment. I want you to go pick something up for me.

—Yes, sir.

By then, the medical people were halfway to the elevators, moving fast under the hard bright light. I turned back for just a second and looked at Max's apartment with the lights on. It was still elegant, rich, a real playpen. And all it had cost her was everything. As I walked out the door, one of the cops must have cranked up the volume on her phonograph.

. . . I wanna be a wise child too . . .

In the ambulance, I told them to go to Sacre Coeur instead of Charity. If Maxine was gonna make it, I wanted her close by. Nothing she'd told me meant a thing if I couldn't get it on paper or tape. Only the physical evidence was going to mean anything, and all that added up to was a very, very bad cop doing awful things to a number of people—for a person or persons unknown.

The rain was still falling, and I could feel that early touch of winter in the air. All that means in New Orleans is three or four months of cold gray overcast skies, leafless trees, people wearing unaccustomed wool. It almost never snows down here. But Maxine shivered under her cotton hospital blanket. She was used to satin comforters, silk sheets.

She came around just for a moment, likely roused by the siren's howl.

—Rat...please...

—What? I asked her.

—Hold...me...

I'm either a dumb ass or a saint. I wouldn't put a dime on either side. But I didn't hesitate. I glanced at the intern riding with us. He shrugged, and I pulled her up into my arms, my lips brushing her hair, her cheek. Her perfume called me back to another rainy night that seemed almost as far away as memory could reach, and we rode that way, the siren crying, for as long a time again.

CHAPTER
11

It was another dawn, and the sun kept trying to break through the clouds. But the rain wouldn't stop falling. The street outside Sacre Coeur was awash, and the trees shuddered and bent away from the waves of rain.

The emergency room was almost empty. The night's long mean pulse had fallen away. The new day's hadn't begun yet. They had Maxine Hawkins in a screened-off cubicle with all the talent in the room working as hard as they could. I reckoned it wouldn't be enough.

I lit a cigar and stared down a young nurse who wanted to tell me to douse it. She started to say something, but that's as far as it went. She frowned and considered and closed her mouth again. I must have looked bad, what with my coveralls torn and dirty, one sleeve ripped away where Wes had bandaged up my shoulder, and the MAC-10 lying on a chair beside me. The bandage had soaked through, and a little blood was running down my arm. I didn't blame the nurse. I'd have kept quiet, too.

As I was trying to ease the pain in my shoulder, my hand brushed across the cosmetics jar in my pocket. I took it out and opened it. Nothing to see. It looked like greasepaint to me. But I knew better. I knew Camille had been right all along. Danny Bynum was clean—so clean he'd pushed the dopers into sending him a message in a jar. It hadn't been hard. They owned Max Hawkins, and she was doing the security detail after working hours. She'd walked into his dressing room before he got to the Superdome, dosed the makeup, and stepped outside again—the for-sure last suspect in the whole damned place. Afterward, in the confusion, she'd picked up the jar of greasepaint and walked away. Piece of cake.

Desire Project and its antidrug campaign must have been hurting them all over the country. I'd underestimated how much effect five kids with instruments could have. Maybe Danny Bynum had been teaching a whole generation that reality is all we've got, that dope dreams all end the same way.

But why hit him in New Orleans? Why not? It was easier here. Because in New Orleans the interplay between legal and illegal is as old as the Black Hand, the Mafia's granddaddy, founded here a hundred years and more ago. Because people here move back and forth across the line the way people move across a West European border nowadays. Because, Miami aside, there's no place else in the country where a hit costs less. Forget it. It happened here because it happened here. I was sure Franco Burnucci had ordered it. My only question was, Did he know he'd hit his own grandson?

I wanted to go upstairs to tell Camille. I wanted her to know her boy was as clean as she believed he was, that however it turned out, he'd gone down like a soldier, not a junkie. Something else: I was going to tell her that we were better than halfway to proving who'd bought the coma for her son.

Just then the young cop who'd been at River Tower

walked in. He handed me Danny's headband and my keys.

—This what you wanted, Captain?

—Right. You finished at Maxine's place?

—Yeah. Didn't turn up much. The lady lived out of suitcases.

—Maybe she knew she wouldn't be there too long.

—I talked to the manager. He said the place was a sublet, rented furnished. Right down to the sheets and kitchenware. None of the stuff was really hers.

I nodded. She'd gotten even less than I thought out of it. Then I handed him the jar of makeup and the headband.

—Put this stuff in a bag and drop it off at Forensics. Tell them I want a check. Is the stuff on the headband the same as in the jar?

—You got it, Captain.

I watched him walk back outside into the rain. Shafts of sunlight were breaking through here and there, and the raindrops sparkled as they fell through the golden light. What was it my momma used to say when it rained in the sunshine? Yeah, the devil's beating his wife. And the devil most usually wins. Momma hadn't told me that part. I learned it on my own.

As I turned back toward the cubicle walled off in hospital gray, the intern who'd ridden with us on the ambulance came out. He shrugged once more, like he had on the way in. We stood there a moment in silence.

—Jesus, she was beautiful, he said finally. —What kind of animal would do that to her?

—I don't know, I said, my voice as steady as if I didn't know.

—When they find him, they ought to tear his balls out, the intern said, his face turning ugly with anger and some special pain of loss. He hadn't been a doctor long enough to be used to it. Good for him.

—Maybe that's already happened, I said, and pushed past him into the cubicle.

The nurses were finishing up and left as I lifted the gray sheet from Max's face. Her eyes were almost closed, but not quite. One corner of her mouth was curled a little, and the effect was as if she'd just heard a really nasty little joke, one she'd never tell. Haven't we all, baby, I thought. Same fucking joke over and over again. We never stop laughing, and we never learn. Most of all, we never tell.

I kissed her cool forehead. I didn't want to leave her there to wait for the pathologists alone, but I had promises to keep. Ones I'd made to myself. One I was making to Max Hawkins right then. In an hour or so, they'd have finished the autopsy, completed the work of destruction my bullets had begun. There'd be a report on the wounds, on major organs, even on her brain tissue. You don't want to know what would be left for her mother to mourn and bury. I wished I didn't know myself.

On the way up to the fourth floor, I kept telling myself I was going to knock on Camille's door, step inside, and spend half an hour apologizing. That might be long enough for me to get my temper under control and figure out the next step and the best way to take it.

But it didn't work out that way. When I came off the elevator, the Bookends down in front of Burnucci's suite were changing shifts. One of them saw me and smiled. He said something under his breath, and the other one just couldn't help grinning, too. When I reached up to knock on the door of Danny's suite, I remembered Max lying on her rented bed like a pile of old clothes someone had set out to be thrown away.

My hand came down, and I walked along the hall to

where Burnucci's people stood.

—Up against the wall, I said. —And spread 'em.

—Hey . . .

—You gonna argue?

—You coon sonofa . . .

He hadn't seen the MAC-10 hanging by my side; and when the receiver caught him in the face, the other one raised his hands, so I just gave him the barrel in his gut as hard as I could. He faded and slid down the wall to the floor. I clipped the first one behind his ear while he was trying to sort out what was left of his mouth. When they were both quiet, I opened the door. The sitting room was empty. Nicky-baby was off sleeping somewhere with someone. I was gonna have the old man all to myself.

I walked in and looked at Franco Xavier Burnucci. If you saw him in a TV commercial or walking down the street, you'd register all-American grandpa. His thin white hair was combed back over a pink scalp, and his mouth was open as he slept lightly under a soft blue-tinted bulb. He was wired to some kind of machine, or maybe three or four. His manicured hands rested on the sheet, a little plastic bracelet ID around one wrist.

I could have been there ten seconds or ten minutes studying him, trying to see some telltale sign that would set him apart from other men who look just like him, who live decent lives, love their families, and do their neighbors no harm. But there was nothing that set him apart. No mark, no sign, no certain look, I was telling myself. Then his eyes snapped open. One moment he was sleeping. Then he was awake. His eyes found mine, and I saw the sign I'd been looking for.

Franco Burnucci's eyes were pale blue and as cold as ice from the asteroid belt. They were hard and sharp and carved across you like laser scalpels. I could see why men did what he told them to do. The will behind those eyes understood nothing at all but obedience. Even then, staring up at a six-foot-four black in filthy coveralls with a bloody shoulder and a machine gun in his hands, there was no hint of fear in his eyes. The loose mouth, the chalky flesh, the sagging cheeks—all of it vanished in the corrosive glare of his eyes. Then I heard his voice for the first time. Like gravel being shaken in a box.

—Who you? he coughed. —Who sent you?

—You don't want to know why?

—You tell me who. I'll know why.

—Camille Bynum, I said. —She wants you dead, shitbag.

So help me God, he smiled. —I don't know her. You gonna do this thing, or you want to deal?

I didn't answer. I was getting my breath.

—Come on, make up you mind. Either I got a day ahead of me, or I don't. What kinda money we talkin'?

—No price. A man who'd hit his own grandson...

He stared at me as if I was the sick one lying in bed. He wasn't pretending. He didn't know what I was talking about. Then he struggled to sit up against his pillows.

—I got no grandson. I got Dominic. That's all I got. Like havin' nothing. Hey, you gonna do what this Camille pay you for? Maybe you hear my confession first.

—Nobody's got that kind of time. The pope couldn't clean you up.

—*Protestante negri,* he laughed. —God see everything, understand. Forgive everything. Why you think he's God?

—You sent Max Hawkins to hit Danny Bynum. Why? Was he cutting into your sales?

Burnucci shook his head and reached for a glass of water.

—You talkin' crazy. Whatsa matter? Nico owe you for a valve job on the Ferarri? Short pay running the numbers? Lemme know what you need.

—Your son had a girfriend twenty years ago . . . Camille Bynum. He did a job on her.

He frowned. —Camille . . . ? I don't know. Maybe something he picked up on the street.

I felt the MAC-10 coming up. I took my finger off the trigger and set it along the receiver. I didn't want it to be an accident when it happened.

—She had a son . . . Nick's son.

Burnucci's eyes narrowed. —Naw . . . Not a chance.

—He's down the hall in another suite. Pumped full of drugs. You sent Hawkins to waste him. The same way Peetie Postum got dropped up in Baton Rouge.

That last name pulled him up short. He did know Peetie. Indeed he did.

—Hey, what's this? His expression changed. He leaned over toward me, his face out of the bluish light.

—I know you, he said. —Trapp. Big black cop . . .

—Maybe I'm off the force, I said. —Maybe I've gone into pest control.

Burnucci made a gesture with his hands. —No, you a cop. You come here to lie, tell me a lot of shit. In the old days, the cops take me in, tie me to a chair. They work me with a rope end all night long in the Third District station house. Shit, they carry me over to Algiers to stay ahead of my lawyer so they can work me in shifts. You know what good? Nothing. I can't walk for a month, but they got . . . nothing. What you think you gonna get?

—Satisfaction, I told him, setting the long silencer against his chest.

There was sweat on his forehead, but the eyes were level and still absolute zero. I knew what he was feeling. The gut has its reasons. The body gets scared even when our brains are too tough or too mean to be.

—You gonna do it, do it.

—My time, not yours, you old bastard. If I had the

stuff, I'd pump you full of dope and watch your eyes melt.

—Watch you own dick fall off, jig.

—You're sweating, Franco.

—You gonna cry when my boys come for you. You dead. You standing there dead.

—What are you gonna tell me about Max Hawkins?

—Never heard of the sonofabitch. Use it or lose it, nigger. They check me every ten minutes.

Come to think of it, I wondered what that nurse who was supposed to be watching the TV monitor was doing. It didn't really matter. Burnucci was right. Whether he didn't know or wouldn't say, I couldn't be sure. But if I'd planned to shake him, I could forget it.

—You got a stay, Burnucci. I like to watch you thinking you're gonna die. You're real strong, old man, but it's an effort. Next time I slap your boys out of the way and come in, it's gonna be harder still . . . and the time after that . . .

His eyes never changed, but I knew I'd hit the only nerve he had. He'd gone hit for hit with me for twelve good rounds. But he knew he didn't have it for the last three. When he was twenty years old, I think he could have taken me. But now he was in his deep seventies. He'd known Costello and Capone, Luciano and Genovese, Lepke and Shultz. Like the young men always say, Move over. Be a legend. Stand in a niche like Florentine marble and smile at us. But move over.

Now the fear of death was on him. Not because he was a coward, but because he was no fool. Burnucci felt himself moving toward the shadows, and he could see waiting for him in a grove of Italian cypress the faces of men he'd killed fifty years ago. Maybe he was praying that there's nothing after death. Because anything there might be wasn't going to be good for him.

—You lousy black...

His face turned to ashes as he tried to come out of the bed after me. He managed to get both feet on the floor, but I pushed him back onto the sheets with the barrel of my piece. He grabbed his chest. For just a second I thought he was bullshitting me.

—You're not gonna die, Franco, I told him. —Not till I say you can.

He tried to say something else, but he couldn't get it out. Then the door burst open and Kenny Amadeo, a doctor with a thin moustache, and a couple of residents pounded into the room.

Amadeo looked angry, but under control, like a snake coiled and ready to strike. —My uncle is in this hospital for tests under a court order from Judge Starke. You have no authority to question him. Now get out, Captain, or I'll see you charged with contempt of court.

The old man and I had done our business, so I gave Amadeo a warm smile and left. Outside, the Bookends were sitting on one of the love seats trying to get their shit together. One was rubbing his neck. The other had a handkerchief over his mouth. They weren't bad boys. They just smelled bad.

When I went behind the counter at the nurses' station, a young nun tried to stop me. I think it was the same one who'd tried to treat me like a truant the first time I visited Burnucci's suite.

—You have no business here...

I ignored her while I looked for the video recorder and the audio line under the bank of monitors. I pulled out the long-play tape that was on and stuck in a blank. On the monitor, I could see the doctor with the moustache giving Franco a shot of something as Amadeo acted solicitous about his uncle's condition. The nun grabbed my shoulder, the one that had the crease in it. I pulled my badge case and slapped it open on her chest.

—Sister, you want to be the first nun to make Orleans Parish Lockup in two hundred and fifty years?

That seemed to cool her. She went back to pushing her papers. You could have launched a plane from her lower lip, but she'd done her duty as God gave her the light to see her duty. What can a helpless nun do against a savage with a badge?

I pushed the taped record of my little talk with Mr. X in the deep utility pocket on my left hip, then walked back to Camille's room. If Amadeo wanted to give me a bad time, he wasn't going to have any video assistance.

The corridor was getting busy. Carts with food were being pushed up and down. Medication was being passed out. An orderly was carrying one of the trays of food into Camille's room. I followed him.

She was sitting next to the window in a big formal chair covered with bright fabric. Outside, the clouds were still heavy except in one place where the sun sliced through and lit up the trees and houses like a shot for an Easter card. She didn't turn when the orderly set her breakfast down and left.

—Take it away, she said softly without turning. —I'm not hungry.

I studied her profile against the clouds outside the window. I wanted to see the girl I'd loved twenty years ago, the one I'd never managed to put out of mind. But it wouldn't happen. I saw a fine-looking woman come back south from California. Nice clothes even at eight-thirty in the morning. Hair just right, a fresh manicure. Nobody I ever knew in Desire project. If I was meeting her for the first time today, I'd be interested. But it wasn't the first time.

She still hadn't turned. —I said you could go, she told the low clouds that had closed out the sun again and started pelting the window with rain once more.

—I just got here, I said.

When she turned, our eyes met. She reached out for me as if we'd never been apart. What the hell, maybe we were meeting for the first time. Maybe every time a man and woman married for thirty years wake up in the same bed and look at each other, they're meeting for the first time. Again.

—Ralph...

—You were right. I was wrong.

—What...?

—Danny...he wasn't using drugs.

Even believing as she had, against me, against everyone, she looked surprised.

—Then...

—Somebody did it to him. The DMSO with heroin and coke dissolved in it was slipped into his stage makeup.

—Why would anyone...

—I think I know, but it's not locked down.

—Who? I want to know...

I think I had meant to tell her what Max had told me, but when I saw the dark circles around her eyes, the lines that grief had etched in her face, I decided not to say anything just yet.

—When I know for sure, you'll know.

She started to say something else. Then she noticed my shoulder for the first time.

—Oh, God...my mind's so tied up with Danny... what happened?

—It's all your fault, I laughed, trying to lift her spirits.

—What?

—I been messing with rough women. Leather clothes, boots, chains...

—I'll bet. I hope you whipped her ass. You need that bandage changed.

—Shit, honey, I need that. I need food. I need sleep. I need friends and money and a good accountant.

That touched her off, and we laughed. But her good cheer didn't last.

—Ralph...

—Yeah?

—I'm glad you're here. Will you come with me? Danny's doctor asked me to come to his office for a... conference. He wants to tell me how Danny's doing.

We held hands all the way to the doctor's office. I gave a quick knock at the door, and the doctor came to open it. It was Richard Lanier, the best neurosurgeon in the state. Maybe the best in the country. I ought to know. He'd sewn me back together twice.

—Mrs. Bynum, he started. Then he recognized me. He saw the shoulder and went to probing at the bloody bandage.

—Goddamnit, Rat... what's this?

I pulled back. I said Lanier was the best, not the tenderest.

—What do you say, Dick? Not a thing. I was just going down to ER to get the bandage changed. You want to let loose of it before I break your wrist?

—Gunshot?

—'Fraid so.

—Don't they ever miss when they shoot at you?

—Size of the target, Doctor. If you can hit a bull in the ass at three feet...

—I asked him to come with me, Camille put in. —It's all right, isn't it, Doctor?

—Rat's a friend of yours, Mrs. Bynum?

—The oldest. The best. And Danny's...

—Fine. That's good.

Dick nodded at me. It was early in the morning and he didn't want to be where he was. He liked me being there to help him out. He liked it a lot.

We pulled our chairs around his mahogany Empire desk. Dick reached in his desk drawer for a bottle and half-filled three water glasses with Remy Martin. I reckoned he didn't have surgery later. More than that, I was sure he had nothing but bad news for Camille.

I don't know about the surgery, but I was right about the news.

—This is the third day, Mrs. Bynum.

—Yes...?

—Ma'am, I'm so very sorry. There's no change. The EEG on Danny is flat. There's just nothing to hope for now.

—But with a little more time...

—It doesn't work that way. Your son is...brain-dead. We could keep him here ten years. The EEG is going to tell us the same thing three hundred and sixty-five days of every one of them.

I took hold of Camille as she tensed and then went limp. There was nothing to hear. She didn't sob and carry on. Maybe that was the only good thing she'd taken from Desire with her. Out there, we cried without a sound. Don't let anyone know you're hurting. That's when they'll do you for sure.

Then her head snapped up. She turned from Dick Lanier to me, and her eyes almost put me in mind of Burnucci's.

—I won't let him go, she rasped. —Not yet. Not now. Don't ask me...

—Mrs. Bynum, Dick began, his voice tired, his words in a pitch I could tell he'd used before. —Mrs. Bynum, Danny's brain is gone. His other organs are functioning mechanically. I think we ought to cut machine support and let his body follow.

—No, Camille almost shouted as she rose from her

chair. —Not now. Not yet. I can't ... I won't ...

I started after her as she ran out, but Dick stopped me. —Give her a little time, Rat.

I considered, then nodded. Maybe she had to be alone to cry.

—Get down to ER and let them take care of that shoulder.

—All right. Then I'll go check on Camille.

—Youall are close?

—We were. Once.

—Stick with her, he said as he walked me to the door. —If you ever were close, now is the time.

CHAPTER
12

In the ER, the intern who had worked so hard on Maxine took care of my shoulder. He was still steaming.

—If they catch the cocksucker, maybe they'd let me pull the switch, he muttered.

I looked at him and tried to remember how it felt to be that young, that intense, that deep into sheer beauty that you wanted to waste anybody who destroyed it. I decided I liked the kid. He was going to hurt one hell of a lot every day of his life. But then he was going to live every one of those days right down to the gristle, too.

—Don't worry about that, Doctor. If anybody pulls the switch on him, it'll be me.

—Yeah? Great. When you do, think of me, huh?

—You can count on it.

He swabbed and powdered and bandaged me, then I headed back to the fourth floor. I tried to think what to say to Camille. Listen to your doctor. The last time Dick Lanier was wrong was in fourth-grade math. I knew she wouldn't want to hear me say Pull the Plug, but what other choice did she have? Only the hope that Danny would save her that decision and go on over even with all mechanical systems in place. That would be the last best gift he could give his mother.

I'm not sure how I expected to find her, but it never occurred to me she'd be in the state she was.

Camille was standing next to Danny's bed, a faint smile on her face, looking as if Dick Lanier had changed his mind. When I saw who was standing close by, I thought I was hallucinating.

Franco Burnucci was wearing an expensive satin robe that didn't fit him anymore, supporting himself unsteadily with both hands on the rail at the foot of the bed. His face was pale and drawn, something left over from my visit, or maybe not. He wasn't paying any attention to either one of us. Not yet. He was still staring down at Danny Bynum's face, illuminated in the small circle of blue light like the one in which I'd seen Burnucci's a little while ago.

—What the hell? I said in a low voice.

His chin came up, and he looked down the length of the bed at me. Then I heard that gravel box he used for a voice. —I got to go back, he said, as if he'd come up from the depths for a visit and his time was running short.

—Mrs. Bynum, if there's anything . . . His voice trailed off, and he shuffled toward the door. As he opened it, he turned back and took one last long look at Danny.

—I got a bad heart, he said softly. —But not so bad as my son's.

I heard Burnucci say that as he closed the door, but I don't think Camille did. When I turned back to her, she was leaning over Danny, smoothing his hair, kissing him carefully—as if she didn't want to wake him.

—What was he doing here?

—It's all right, she said.

—Why? Why is it all right? That sonofabitch . . .

—Don't talk like that. He's just an old man from down the hall. He came to visit Danny.

To look at his glossy blue-black hair, his high cheekbones, his smooth dark olive skin. I hadn't scared the old man worth mentioning, but I'd scored just the same.

—Did he say anything?

—Just he came to . . . pay respect, offer his sympathy. He said he hoped Danny would come around. I told him Danny won't be coming around, Camille said softly, with great dignity, from a place far away. —That my son is . . .

Her voice broke, and I put my arms around her. She wore a different perfume now, but the skin, the hair reminded me.

—Don't you know who that was? I asked. She shook her head without lifting it from my shoulder.

—Franco Burnucci, Nick's father.

Her head snapped up at that. —Franco . . . That nice old man? But why . . .

—I guess he came to visit his grandson, I told her.

—Rat, you're wrong . . .

I guess she couldn't believe how age had almost worn him away. —It's him all right. Your . . . near-miss father-in-law.

—Rat, there's something you have to know . . .

Whatever it was she meant to tell me got stopped in her throat. There was a quick peremptory knock at the door, and a nurse came in. It was the one who'd ordered me away from the desk a couple of hours before. She came in with her eyebrows in a straight line and did a little take with her shoulders aimed straight at me.

—You have a phone call, Captain. They say it's urgent.

—I'll take it at the nurses' station.

I hugged Camille and left. I didn't like going. I could tell she was still in shock, still not ready to believe that Danny and Desire Project had gone the way everything from the projects always went. But all I could do for her now was get Burnucci.

It was Mauvais. He was sounding somewhere close to DEFCON 4, saying I'd finally gone right off the Greater Mississippi River Bridge. Nobody could cover for me on this one. My career was history.

—Cover for me? Shit, when in the hell did you people do anything but ride me ragged? You been covering for me? I must have missed a beautiful moment.

—Get in here. Now. That's an order.

—Yassah...Massah...

—You smart-mouthed son of a black...

—Don't say it, Mauvais. We know each other too well.

It was a failure of communication, a cognitive disjunction, as they say at the FBI Academy. Mauvais and I had this basic dissonance stemming from the fact that we could hardly stand living on the same planet—much less in the same town. I was doing army time while he was emptying wastebaskets, shuffling and nosing his way up the bureaucratic pile. You understand the problem. Or you don't.

The hell with him and the rest of them. I was hungry and tired. I couldn't do much about the tired, but I could fix up the hungry. When I got to Tulane and Broad, I stopped by Denise's place and grabbed a handful of the DA's office Danish and some coffee.

—Oh, boy, she said, staring at me with wide beautiful eyes.

—You got any brandy? I asked her. —For the coffee.

—No. God, I'm glad you peeled Wes off before you went into high gear last night.

—I'll bet he's not glad.

—He's dying. He's out there following your trail all the way from Desire to River Tower to Sacre Coeur. Good God, Rat...

—We don't hand down judgments till we've had a trial, do we, counselor?

—I don't know. Maybe that's not efficient. I mean, two dead—one of them a cop. What about Maxine Hawkins?

—Hawkins blew away Peetie Postum . . . and your case-in-chief, dolly.

She looked as if I'd dropped Utah on her.

—You're not serious.

—Never more. She was on Burnucci's payroll. We got the rifle. A cop found it at her place.

—Ballistics?

—In progress. You ought to have a report in a couple of hours. But take my word.

Denise looked somber, shook her head. —Then you can quit blaming yourself. She didn't follow you to Baton Rouge.

—You're right. Max was one of the officers working shifts guarding Peetie.

—I guess you never know about people.

—Don't it make you want to go home? Then she offed Tyrone last night.

—Uh-uh. That's not the way I heard it. That apartment was all shot to hell—with a MAC-10. Like the one that . . . you know . . .

I realized what made her voice go low. The gun I'd taken from police Property was one she remembered well. She should have. It had killed her grandfather.

—Autopsy's gonna show he died of three .38 Specials in the heart—delivered before the 9mms hit him. The MAC-10 was mine.

—But, Rat, why would you . . .

—Denise, Hawkins was shooting at me. I just let go every whichaway . . . and Tyrone couldn't move.

—Postum and Jefferson . . . some lady cop.

—She did Danny Bynum, too.

That stopped Denise's musings cold. She studied me as if she was trying to decide whether I was a joker or a lunatic.

—Captain, this is business. You know that.

I couldn't help laughing a little. Amidst all the pain and horror, the outrageous still shimmied right on through.

—Counselor, I know it's business. I'm telling you the rock-bottom truth. I know it's harder to swallow down than this damn Danish of yours. Would you rather hear it from Forensics? I mean, would that work for you better? They're checking out some stage makeup Max had sitting on a shelf next to a bottle of DMSO. Remember she worked Security at the Dome the night of the concert.

I could see I hadn't made her day. But once she got used to all the crap I was laying on her, she was going to feel better. We'd come a long way from a couple of dead pushers. She kept her eyes down on her desk for a moment or two and then looked up at me. Smiling. Lord, if Wes Colvin doesn't do right by that girl...

—I'm sorry, Rat, she said. —I really am. But... why Danny?

I remembered Burnucci's gray face as he stared down at Danny, having just heard from Camille he'd never rise up from that hospital bed. What had the old man felt? Relief? Regret?

—I don't know for sure. Max didn't live long enough to answer me that.

I timed it so I'd hit Mauvais's office about eleven-thirty. He'd keep me waiting ten minutes, rave and tear the carpet for ten minutes, try to reason with me for ten minutes, then he'd give it up so he wouldn't be late for lunch down at Arnaud's. I've always got me a plan.

Some plans work better than others. His secretary ran me through the outer office like I was a bag of plasma at a disaster. Mauvais was behind his desk. Kenny Amadeo, Burnucci's nephew, was patting his five-hundred-dollar suit down like he thought he might have something strong in one of his pockets. He found himself a cigarette and lit it as he stared out at a view of downtown. I noticed the rain had cleared away, but the clouds still hung around. The rain would be back later.

—We've been waiting almost an hour, Captain, Mauvais grated, staring at me like some of the old white boys used to do.

—I'm so sorry, I said. —I had to stop in the ER and get my bandages changed.

—Before or after you stopped by to visit Mr. Burnucci?

—Let me see. As I recall...

—You admit you entered his room?

—I was passing by. The door was open, and I...

Amadeo smiled. I could see why there were rumors he could be the next *capo* instead of his cousin Nick. Very capable, very cool. Virgina Law, Wharton School of Finance. He must have fit right in. Kenny's not a lawbreaker like his uncle. He's a lawbender. Lawbreakers go to jail—sometimes. Lawbenders go to the board of directors—always. If he ever did take things over in New Orleans, crime might get organized. Not nicer, not cleaner, but smarter, much smarter. If I was naming *capos*, I'd rather put Nick Burnucci in. He'd be scared shitless from day one. I could keep him in permanent panic. Amadeo? I don't know.

—The Malaporte brothers are in the emergency room now. Santo is going to need orthodontic surgery.

—Ah, I said. —Those two felons I found messing around in the corridor...

Amadeo started to say something, but Mauvais cut him off. —I don't want you in Sacre Coeur while Burnucci is there, he barked.

—Well, you see, Major, I've got a case working there.

—What case?

—The Danny Bynum situation.

—The singer who overdosed?

—*Was* overdosed.

—What are you talking about?

I could see Amadeo was listening. Maybe for the first time.

—I don't want to go into details in public, Major.

—I want you to.

—No.

Mauvais studied me, then shrugged. He turned to Amadeo.

—You have my assurance Captain Trapp won't be bothering Mr. Burnucci again. Will that do, Mr. Amadeo?

Kenny smiled as he rose and slipped his Florentine-leather briefcase under his arm. It was a beautiful piece— so long as you didn't want to put more than three sheets of paper in it. But then, it was a prop. Kenny wasn't a lawyer. He was a *consigliere*. He hired legal talent the way you and I might hire yardmen.

—Of course, Major, he said, —Your word is always good with us. Gentlemen...

Amadeo walked out. I was thinking what it meant to have him say Mauvais's word was always good with... us. Who exactly was us? And how come Mauvais's word was so damned good with them? I knew the answer to the first question. Maybe before I opened all the doors and pulled the trash out into the light, I'd know the answer to the second question.

Mauvais came back from seeing Amadeo to the door.

—All right. I want to know your case on the Bynum thing.

—Hawkins dosed his greasepaint with a speedball dissolved in DMSO so it'd be carried through the kid's skin when he put on his stage makeup. The dope caused a coronary arrest.

—Horseshit. When I heard the poor girl was dead, I told myself, she's going to catch every piece of bad news second-rate police work can put on her.

—You lie to yourself like that all the time? Don't answer. I know.

—She shot Postum. She shot Jefferson. She shot you. She doped this Bynum kid. What about the Kennedys and Dr. King?

—If I could place her there, I'd give you six to one across the board. Max played rough.

Mauvais nodded. —The ballistics fit on Postum and Jefferson. Did they pull a slug out of you?

—It's in the floor out where Tyrone bit it.

—What evidence ties her to the Bynum case?

—The lab has the kid's headband and a jar of stage makeup I found at her place. I found a bottle of DMSO. I don't know if they turned up the coke and smack or not.

—They did, Mauvais gritted. —A couple of bags taped under the night table. Top grade pure, uncut.

I sympathized with his pain. If he'd been out there on the job, going over Maxine's apartment, they'd have never found a thing. They might have missed her body.

—Why? Mauvais asked.

—I'm working it. Max told me she worked for Burnucci. She owed him.

—Owed him what?

—She had three slugs in her. She wasn't chatty. She said she'd sent Tyrone on his way to set me up because . . . I knew everything.

—You . . . knew everything? Mauvais repeated. —You were a witness to the old man's talk with Peetie Postum, but with Postum dead, your testimony wouldn't . . .

—You're missing it, I told him. —I think Max meant I knew too much about the Bynum kid.

—What do you know?

—Danny Bynum's . . . , I started to say.

Then I shrugged. Why start pitching before the umpire yells "Play ball"? I had to know more than I did to know anything at all—much less everything.

—The kid's brain-dead, I said. —They want to take him off life support. That's what pushed me to roust Burnucci. The sonofabitch sent Hawkins to do the kid. I'm gonna nail it on his ass.

Mauvais was fixing to start ripping on me again when one of his assistants came in and dropped a piece of paper on his desk.

—Well, shit, he said, his jaw dropping in surprise.

I thought it must be a national defense alert. Mauvais normally has the metabolism of a toad in deep winter.

He looked up at me. —You can forget Franco Burnucci, he said. —He just died at Sacre Coeur.

CHAPTER
13

We all got to go sometime, Eddie Lombard was telling me as we rode up to the fourth floor of Sacre Coeur with Mauvais. —The old man's heart was Swiss cheese.

—How do you know? I asked him.

—I ran an EKG on him when he came in. —Chest full of dogshit. Arrhythmia, lungs collecting fluid, lots of angina.

He stopped and frowned. —You know, he must have been hurting all the time. He never let on.

Mauvais was glaring at me as he spoke to Eddie. —Could an argument, somebody coming into his room, hassling him...?

Eddie laughed. —Listen, a fly lighting on his nose could have. But it wouldn't matter. Cause of death was his fucking heart caved in. We all got to...

—Ummm, Mauvais grunted. He wasn't talking much. He was already stroking his way through the administrative hearing that was gonna bust my ass. In his imagination.

When we hit the fourth floor, it was full of people. There was Amadeo with the Malaporte Bookends right beside him. They were all looking devastated. A bunch of other goons were milling around, shaking Amadeo's hand like a decision had already been made. It hadn't, but they'd be fixing the succession soon.

Medical people kept going in and out of Burnucci's suite. I don't know who had put the uniformed cops outside the door. Sister Mary Cecilia came up to me.

—Captain Trapp...

—Sister, are you going to give me a hard time? About this morning?

She looked surprised. —Why, no. I was just going to tell you...

Wes Colvin came up to me. He didn't mean to be rude, but he kind of elbowed his way past the good sister.

—Excuse me, Sister. Can I see you a minute, Rat?

Wes was looking like he knew something. We moved off to one side.

—What have you got? I asked him.

—He's dead.

I reckoned there had to be something to that. —What have *you* got?

—I got me a nurse's aide who heard a slam-bang argument going on in the room. Just before all Burnucci's whizbangs lit up at the nurses' station.

—With who? I asked him.

—Nice-looking middle-aged man. Dark hair, expensive suit. She didn't know him. She's only working the floor today.

—Ummmm. It wasn't Amadeo. He didn't have time to get here from Central Lockup. Anyhow, Kenny never argues with anybody...least of all the old man.

—Ah...Nick.

—Maybe. Where *is* Nick?

—I don't know. Maybe he's on his way.

Then it hit me. Whoever it *was*, I should have him in living color. I broke loose from the crowd and sprinted for the nurses' station. Wes stayed on my elbow. He can always tell when I'm in full cry.

That same damned nurse was there, giving me her Look of Disapproval. When I had all this behind me, I thought I might ask her out. I was sure I had something she'd approve of.

I looked at the monitor. It showed Burnucci's room filled with people. A sheet covered the bed, and two or three orderlies were getting ready to move what was under it onto a gurney. As they lifted their burden, a corner of the sheet fell away.

Franco Xavier Burnucci looked no grayer, no less healthy in death than he had in life. His face was composed, his jaw clamped shut, his eyes closed. There was no trace of rage or fear or remorse on that face. He had done his last day the way he had done his days for over seventy years. The way he'd told Peetie to lose Wee-Wee and Murphy. The way he'd told Maxine to do Peetie, Tyrone, Danny Bynum, and me. Nothing personal. Just business. There weren't going to be any more like him. From now on, it would be slick and automated, clever and circuitous. No more Moustache Joes, no more Castella Marici Wars. I guessed that was good. But then you never know. Maybe the good days were behind us.

They covered him again and wheeled him out. I rolled back the tape to see how Mr. X had taken his last fall.

Wes and I fooled with it, running it back and forth till we found Franco Burnucci lying in bed, looking restlessly out at the leaden skies over the city. I skipped ahead, and, sure enough, there was Nick Burnucci coming into the room. The old man ignored his greeting. You could see Nick's face harden, the cords in his neck tighten as if his father could twist them to the breaking point by nothing more than his silence. Then the audio cut in.

—Poppa, Nick started. —Something's wrong?

—Fuckin' A, something wrong.

—Dino told me about Trapp. He hurt Santo. Did he...?

—Fuck Santo. They got a kid down the hall. They say he's gonna die.

—Uh...

—You know the kid, huh?

—No. How do I know some nigger rock star?

—You known his momma. A long time ago.

—No...

—Don't lie, you shit. One of them coons you pick up in the projects.

—No. Who told you...

—I know when you lie. I smell it on you. Like a barn-yard.

—Poppa, I never...

—You never give me a grandson. You tell me your wife can't carry. I tell you fine, so go where you need to go, but get some family.

—Yeah, well, sometimes...

—Sometimes twenty years ago, this spade you pull out of Desire has a kid, huh? A black kid...my grandson.

Nick looked like he was gonna throw up. He was half-turned away from Franco, and you wouldn't have wanted to see the craziness, the old horrors passing across his face. Either he's a steer—or he's got him a jigaboo son he never mentioned to Dad. Wes and I watched to see which he feared most. His eyes caught fire, and he whirled around to face his father. Maybe for the first time in his life.

—Yeah, a black kid. Mine. The only kid I ever had.

—You screwin' everything it fits, but only one kid in

thirty years, Franco sneered at him. —And him a...

—I took care of it, Nick cut him off. —I sent somebody. We don't have to worry.

—You... You button that kid down the hall? The old man looked stunned. —Jesus, what you do?

And there it was. All this time I had thought Maxine worked for Franco. But she'd gone for the white Cadillac, too. Franco hadn't ordered a hit on his grandson by mistake or any other way.

—Rat, that means Nick Burnucci..., Wes whispered to me.

—Right. And we got it on tape. Hush. Listen...

Nick had been tough for as long as he could make it. Sweat was running down his face. His eyes looked like pinballs in a machine being tilted by a giant.

—I made a mistake. A long time ago. I... sent her away with the kid... to L.A. I told her you hated jigs. I said you'd have her and the kid both popped if she didn't go.

Franco still stared at Nick like he was a more threatening stranger than I had been. Maybe the old man had a premonition. Nick's hands were shaking. He grabbed hold of the bedrail to get them under control.

—But the nigger bastard came back... singing about looking for his father. Can you beat that, Poppa? Looking for me. Wanting to know me. And him a rock star. I knew the press would jump on it. And too much shit's happened already. We've been in the headlines enough. More publicity'd wreck the business. So I sent him a hug and a kiss.

—You hit the kid? You hammer the poor fucking kid?

—For you, Poppa. For the family. What if he'd called some kind of press conference and said he was a Burnucci? We'd have been shit... A *capo*'s gotta have respect.

—You no *capo*, Dominic. Not now. Not ever.

—I know I've messed up before, Poppa. But this time I did it right. The hit looked like an OD. And if anyone asks questions, the hitter's dead.

Franco looked at Nick as if he'd found something filthy on his shoe. His jaw tightened. His eyes turned to granite.

—The scumbag kills . . . my grandson.

Franco picked up his bedside phone and dialed. His movements were clipped, precise. As if his anger had carved away the years and given him back his strength for one last go.

—Poppa . . .

—Hello, Bartolomeo? Tell Kenny I want him here. Now. Huh? Call his car phone. No, I don't give a shit about the black cop. The black cop tells me the truth.

—Poppa . . . ?

—It's over for you, Dominic, hear me? You got the club. That's it. Get out and don't come back. I don't want you face in front of me.

—For God's sake, Poppa . . .

—Everyone tell me you no good, but you my blood. I forgive you. Even the indictment. But now, I got no son. All I got is a nephew.

—You're gonna do this to me? Because of a . . . nigger bastard?

The old man came up from his pillows like a rattler. He slapped Nick across the face. He still had some stuff left. Nick spun around like he'd been brushed by an eighteen-wheeler.

—Not because you got him. Because you kill him. My grandson, Franco rasped, turning his face away from Nick, looking out the window where the clouds had broken for a moment and let shafts of sunlight touch the city here and there. Then he lay back against the pillows, his mouth sagging, that last burst of strength gone.

—Get outta here, he said, still turned away from Nick. —Before I tell Bartolomeo to drop you in the river. Who can trust a man kills his...

It happened so fast that Wes and I both recoiled from the monitor. Nick rushed back into the picture, jerked a pillow from under the old man, and slammed it down over his face. It must have taken him thirty, forty-five seconds to do the thing. Then, when he was done, shaking, falling across the foot of the bed, his eyes came up and fixed on the camera that had caught it all.

—Oh, God, Nick moaned, his father's eyes, frozen in death, drilling into his back. —Oh, Joseph and Mary...

As if he was talking to Wes and me, and knew there was no mercy in us.

—The lousy sonofabitch, Wes breathed. —First his kid. Then... his own father.

I snapped off the monitor, and rolled back the tape. Then I called down the hall to Mauvais. A couple of news people followed him.

—Stay outside the desk area, I told them. I gave Wes a look. He smiled and went outside with the others. For about ten seconds. Then he was gone, headed for a phone. He was going to have a clean beat on this one.

I told Mauvais what was on the tape. He looked like he couldn't believe it.

—Who told you to tape? he asked.

—Who the fuck cares? I've got Nick Burnucci admitting he sent Max Hawkins for the kid—and killing the old man on camera.

—Jesus... I can't believe it. But if you didn't have a warrant...

—I did. Denise Lemoyne got it a couple of days ago.

Mauvais surprised me. He smiled. —She did? Then we're...

—Home free, I finished for him as I handed him the

tape. —Don't forget to mark it, Major. Chain of custody and all that crap.

—What are you going to do?

—Now you *got* to know the answer to that.

But first I stopped at Danny's suite. Camille would want to know. That nurse I'd seen the first time answered the door. She hadn't gotten any better looking.

—Mrs. Bynum...

—Not here.

—Huh...?

—I said...

—I heard what you said. Where'd she go? Down to the coffee shop?

Just then Sister Mary Cecila turned up beside me again. She was frowning, looking concerned.

—Mrs. Bynum isn't in the hospital, Captain. That's what I was trying to tell you when that young reporter...

I looked down at her, trying to make out what she could mean.

—She...left Danny alone?

—I think she was...very upset.

—Yeah, I know. Dick Lanier told her...

—No, something beside that.

—I don't...

—Dr. Lanier asked me to be with her. I suggested we go down to the chapel and pray for guidance.

—That's kind, Sister.

—But the floor nurse asked me to step in her office a moment. She wanted me to carry some property belonging to a new patient down to the safe. Mrs. Bynum waited for me by the monitors. As I came back with the envelope, Mr. Burnucci, Dominic Burnucci, came running out of his father's room.

—Ah...yeah, I can understand that.

—Mrs. Bynum caught up to him in the elevator. They
... stared at each other. It was almost as if they were
acquainted.

—Uh-huh...

—"I saw," she said. No, she didn't *say*. She... she
screamed it at him. "On the monitor, I saw..."

Right then, I got this feeling in my gut. Low down and
cold and twisting.

—Sister, what...

—He looked... terrified. He stepped in the elevator...
and pulled Mrs. Bynum in after him. They...

I didn't need to hear any more. I was already running.
Downstairs, I was in my car before it hit me. I didn't
know where Nick Burnucci would go. He was the hottest
property in Louisiana just then. I could hear the traffic
on my car radio. Mauvais had put out an APB on him.
Maybe Kenny Amadeo and his buddies had heard. If they
hadn't, they would soon. Then it was gonna be a race to
see who put little round holes in Nick-baby first.

As far as I was concerned, I'd have been happy to let
the family take care of its own internal affairs—except
for one thing. When the shooting started, Camille Bynum
was going to be only a foot or two from the center of the
bull's-eye. Cop or Wop, nobody was gonna take the first
shot himself to keep her from getting hurt. That's how
they wrote the Doomtown rules, don't you see?

I tried to settle my mind as I drove out of the Sacre
Coeur parking lot. It wasn't easy. I was dog-tired, still
hungry, and my shoulder felt a lot worse than it really
was. My eyes were blurring on me, and my hands weren't
steady. Nick wasn't smart, but he was mean and dangerous. Wherever Franco was cooking and smoking now,
I'd bet a pound bag of cracklins he wished he'd passed
on having a son. Sometimes it just don't work out.

All right: Nick wasn't going home. Anyhow, all the cops

in Lakeside would be out there going through his closets, his files, his nifty suits. He wasn't going to Vegas East, either. He knew what I knew. If the cops didn't find him there, his cousin Kenny was certain to. From Nick's point of view, better the cops. As I sifted through the possibilities, I couldn't come up with a place he could go where either we or they wouldn't come down on him like a glacier on the Ice Age.

Except one place. I wheeled around and headed Uptown toward River Tower. Maxine's place. It wouldn't be safe for long—maybe not for long enough. But the cops had finished their investigation, and maybe Kenny and his people wouldn't tumble to it before Nick got done with Camille and bought himself a passage to Brazil or some other place where you go when things have gone to hell back home.

He'd have a key to the apartment and a fresh new bill for the downstairs security man. Fine. I had that bastard roped, reined in, and ready to graze. If I'd given him the creeps the night before, this time I was gonna turn his hair gray.

Maxine's apartment was on the river side of the Tower, but I skipped the lot, and pulled into the parking garage real slow. My eyes got accustomed to the dark, and I coasted toward a slot near the elevator. That's when I saw it. Pulled into a space barely big enough to hold it, sleek and sparkling—like the reincarnation of one that had broken my heart twenty years ago. A big white Cadillac Fleetwood.

When I was parked, I picked up my service revolver from under the front seat. This wasn't one of my celebrated rousts, and I thought maybe I'd used the MAC-10 enough this go-round. I pushed the .357 into the belt of my coveralls and eased over by the Cadillac. The windows were opaque. Even the windshield was one-way glass. Nick liked his privacy. I opened the driver's door with my pistol ready. The car was empty. No sign it hadn't been parked for a week—except that the hood was still warm.

I took care of that. It wouldn't be getting warm again soon. Not with the ignition wires ripped out and in my pocket. I hit the garage elevator at a trot. No good. It was a lock elevator, and they'd built it with bad guys like me in mind. The control plate was countersunk in concrete. I could jigger it, but I didn't have a cement chisel and two hours to fool around. I hit the stairs.

There was a different security type in the lobby. But it didn't matter. They're all trained the same. They pull down maybe two fifty a week, but, like the czar's footmen, they sure know how to frown down on guys in torn coveralls.

—Deliveries in back, he told me.

I laid my badge cover on his desk and gave him a smile he didn't deserve. I wrote a phone number on the clean paper in his neat clipboard. He looked like I'd hurt him.

—I'm gonna say this once, right?

—You're . . . a cop?

—I want you to call this number. Tell 'em Trapp's at River Tower. Tell 'em it looks like Nick Burnucci's upstairs in . . . Yeah, 1533.

The guy had his eyes glued on me. I thought maybe he had me mixed up with Wilt Chamberlain. Wrong again. He had me down pat.

—Jesus, you're the cop who killed Miss Hawkins.

—Right. And the day's not over yet. Shut up and listen. Tell 'em to come silent and close this place off, but not to move. Say Burnucci's got Camille Bynum with him. Have you got all that, or do I twist your head off and stuff it up your dying butt?

You'd be surprised how good he had it. He was punch-

ing buttons when I started up in that transparent elevator.
The rain had started again. I looked at my watch. It was
past four, and with the clouds moving in it looked like
dusk.

Did you ever get this terrible feeling that you've been
judged and condemned and nobody had bothered to tell
you? That your punishment had begun, and there was
nothing complicated to it? You were gonna go through
all the events of your life over and over again in infinite
dumb variations—forever.

Like now I was in this goddamned elevator again with
rain slapping against the plastic panels. Like that white
Cadillac down in the parking basement that was almost
as dark as Desire. Like Nick Burnucci had Camille Bynum.
Only this time he might be taking her life instead of just
her body.

I pulled a deep breath and got off when the little light
read 15. Now I was here, I couldn't figure how the hell
I was gonna get in. Then it hit me. There was a balcony.
Right outside that big double sliding-glass door, there was
a balcony. I didn't know how deep or wide, but all the
apartments had balconies. It wasn't the golden key to
certain success, but it was gonna have to do.

I rang the chimes at 1531 and waited with my badge
out. Nothing. Nobody. Probably half the building was
empty, the occupants still at work. I sprinted down to
1535 and gave it another try. If I had to go at 1533 head-
on, somebody was sure to get killed. The odds were looking a lot like me.

But then maybe he'd already done Camille. He had
nothing to lose. Amadeo and the family knew by now
that he'd snuffed Don Franco. The cops knew he had
Camille. Why not shove her out the window? Wait a minute. I knew why not. Nick-baby didn't want to die. He
was using the phone in Max's apartment, trying every

number he knew to buy himself a trip out. And he needed her. With her, he might get by the cops. Not past Kenny and the boys, but that was another problem. The mob's not sentimental. Maybe they'd let him walk if he left the country—or maybe they'd just as soon waste him in Brazil as in the U.S.A. Who gives a shit who you kill in South America?

I heard something behind the door of 1535. My luck was changing.

When she opened the door, she was sixty, in a negligee that revealed much too much about what time can do to a woman's body. She had orange hair and was carrying a Boston bull older than Moses. The thing smelled like it had died and been stuffed by an unskilled taxidermist.

—I don't need none, she told me.

I was relieved. —Police business, ma'am. I need to use your...

—This ain't no public toilet in here.

—...balcony.

That intrigued her. —Whatta you gonna do with my balcony? I mean, like what would a cop need with my...

She squinted at my badge, then back up at me. —You don't look like a cop. You gonna do something filthy on my balcony?

If I did, she'd watch. —Ma'am, there's a crazed killer in the next apartment. More police units are on the way.

Her eyes turned into billiard balls. —You're...swap?

—Huh?

—Swap team, right?

—Uh, yeah. You got it.

—What do I do?

—I'm going from your balcony to 1533. You call downstairs and tell the man at the desk what's happening. Tell him to let the other units know. Can you do that?

The bulldog was struggling in her arms. Like it had

come back from the dead to check out the excitement. Every time it thrashed around, that stench kind of billowed up and out. As I walked into the apartment, the odor was unreal. There was newspaper all over the floor.

—Boston Club's getting old. He ain't got any control.

—He's not the only one.

—Yeah, you know. I watch the TV. Somebody killed an old man in the hospital today. You believe his own son?

—Yeah, I guess I would.

—Fucking bastard. I'm glad I didn't have any kids.

I opened the sliding doors and managed to get outside. I took a deep breath. Boston Club's smell seemed to fade away. The rain whipped around my face, fresh and chill. When I looked down at the parking lot fifteen floors below, I could see mist swirling down there. I wondered if any of my people had made it yet. The hell with it. I wasn't gonna yell down, and they weren't gonna send up a flare. For the next few minutes, I was solo.

The balcony of 1533 was about four feet from the one I was standing on. Close enough to barely reach, but too far for comfort. In the movies, the cop would jump for it. In real life, he'd fall fifteen stories and have his backbone sticking out of his ears.

—Ma'am, I called back behind me, —you got a ladder or anything I can lay across to the next...

She stepped out and took a look.

—You can't jump that?

—Jesus, lady...

The last time I'd got a look like that was from a sergeant. In Ranger training. When I broke my leg. She shook her head.

—No ladder. But I got a board for my back.

She sure enough did. When I pulled it out from under her mattress, I could see that it was long enough. I wasn't gonna walk the damned thing, just use it for support.

When I started over, the old lady was standing on her balcony. The bulldog was at her feet, and he was pissing against the metal uprights that held the balcony rail. If anyone was standing right below, a hard rain was gonna fall.

I came over the rail in a hurry and hunched down as low as I could get. I couldn't see anything but a soft light showing through the gauzy drapes that covered the sliding-glass doors with their frosted leaves and birds. The best break I had was knowing how the room was set up. The sofa was just a couple of feet inside, its back toward the balcony. The phone was on the endtable where the lamp sat. I checked my .357, and the PPK I had stuffed in the upper of my boot hours ago at home and never used. I tried the sliding door, knowing it would be shut and locked. I was gonna have to go through it. It was tempered glass, and I wasn't sure I could kick it in. I decided not to take a chance. I'd put a round through it close to the lock and see what that got me.

But I wanted to know more about what was going on inside. I couldn't hear anything. I couldn't see a damned thing but light from the lamp playing on the eternal frosted face of that wood nymph carved in the window who kept looking like Maxine.

Was Camille in the bedroom? Or did Nick have a death-grip on her? Was he using the phone, or pacing, or staring around the apartment where he'd enjoyed Max Hawkins before he threw her away on a suicide mission? Was waiting gonna get me anything I didn't already have? I decided not. But then, just as I raised the .357 and drew a bead on the lock of the sliding door, I heard the phone inside chuckle. The sound was faint, but I had heard it before.

—Answer it, motherfucker, I prayed. —Do it now, and catch the one in the parlor, not the bedroom extension.

The sound stopped, and I heard a muffled voice I couldn't quite recognize for sure, saying, "Yeah . . . ?"

I fired, and the glass dropped in two or three sheets like ice off a wall. I didn't have to bother with the lock. I was into the drapes where they parted and out of them. Nick Burnucci had the phone in one hand and that damned Uzi machine gun cradled in the other arm.

CHAPTER
14

Nick dropped the phone and cut loose at me with the Uzi. I fired back and took a dive behind the sofa. I might as well have had a Kleenex between me and him. The bullets came through without a pause, ripping padding out of the sofa in chunks. He didn't quite have the angle, but he was tearing up the floor and metal balcony behind me pretty good. I stuck the .357 under the sofa and fired a couple more times. Hitting him in the foot or leg didn't seem very heroic, but nobody can be beautiful all the time.

Then the shooting stopped. I could hear him breathing, and I knew he could hear my heart beating. Down maybe three feet from where I was sprawled, I could see the cord that powered the lamp by the sofa. I wondered if I should give it a pull and see what happened. I couldn't lose. The only situation worse than this was dead.

I made a motion toward crawling, but her voice stopped me cold.

—Ralph . . . please . . . don't let him hurt you.

—Come on up, Trapp. I got the Uzi in her ear. I'm so fucking nervous...

I'd come up his ass. Nick-baby had nothing whatever to lose. Don Franco's had been a capital murder under Louisiana law. I knew it, and he knew it. When a jury heard what he'd been doing just prior to killing his father, why he'd killed his father, it was gonna be a gimme. The only way he'd be leaving Angola was imitating a chicken-fried steak. Cutting me in two when I stood up might be the last pleasure he had in this life.

On the other hand, maybe he'd like two hostages instead of one. No, on the other hand he wouldn't. He could handle Camille. He wasn't gonna risk dicing with me. If I stood up, outlined against the wet fading afternoon, I was blood pudding. I used to eat the stuff in Germany. It was all right, but I wouldn't want to be one.

Just then, something broke into my calculations. I could hear a voice coming faintly from way down below.

—...Dominic Burnucci...building is surrounded. Throw down your weapons and come out. Release Mrs....

—You nigger bastard, Nick screamed at me. —You brought the whole fucking...

—Yeah, well, I thought I'd need 'em. To keep Kenny Amadeo and his boys off you.

—What?

—We recorded your act, Nick-baby. There you are, killing your old man on TV.

—You...recorded...oh, Jesus...

—Hell, maybe that's not even the cops down there. Maybe the family pitched in and got 'em a bullhorn from American Rent-All.

Nick didn't think it was funny. He sent another blast my way. If he got any closer, I was gonna have me a lead-lined ass. Cotton floated down on my nose, and the last glass panel of the door blew out. Down below, it was gonna be sofa stuffing, chunks of plate glass, and dog piss. Come to think, maybe I was better off up here.

I heard Nick mumble something to Camille, then her voice came at me again.

—Ralph . . . Nick just wants to walk out of here, leave the country. Let him go. I don't want to see him kill you, too.

—Oh, baby, neither do I. But even if we forget about the old man, Peetie, Tyrone . . . Danny deserves more than that.

—Danny? What does he . . . ?

—Shut up, Trapp, Nick yelled. Then I heard the door to the hallway open. I'd let him get clear and then take my best shot. He wasn't gonna make the parking garage or the lobby alive. I don't know that I was up on dying for Camille. But Nick Burnucci wasn't gonna take her off again. Losing her to that dago bastard twice the same way was out. We all draw lines somewhere, sometime. I was drawing mine right then.

When I heard the hollow sound of their voices arguing in the hall, I came up over the sofa and took a running dive at the door. As I got there, the frame turned into splinters and dust. Down the corridor, near the elevators, I could see Nick standing, moving the submachine gun side to side.

Camille was yelling at him. —What did he mean about Danny? Tell me . . .

I took a head shot at Nick and missed. The slug splintered plastic above him, and he let go at me again.

This time I was on the floor when plaster and pieces of light fixture from up above came raining down. Then I was up and moving. Because the elevator had arrived, and as it opened, Nick started dragging Camille inside. She looked back at me, her face stiffened in hopelessness and outrage at Burnucci adding this thing to all he'd done to her before.

I was running then, firing three more shots, knowing I couldn't hit him at that distance, in that light, on the move. I didn't realize my weapon was empty till the sound of the hammer snapping on spent rounds came to me. I hit the floor and skidded into the wall opposite the elevator doors that were closing. There was no way I could stop him.

I reached down and pulled the PPK from my boot and slid it across the smooth carpet and into the elevator car.

—Camille, he did it. The sonofabitch killed Danny, I yelled as Burnucci aimed the Uzi point-blank at me and fired one last time as the doors closed.

It was as if somebody had hit me in the side with a two-by-twelve plank. I kind of oozed onto the carpet trying to get my breath, trying to find out if I had any breath left. Then I saw that the other elevator had arrived and stood with its doors open.

I got to my feet, dropped back to my knees, then some way or other got myself into the elevator. I pounded on the down button with one fist while the other was twisted into the right side of my coveralls, trying to hold back the dull throb that was going to turn to lightning and acid in a moment or two—as soon as my body found out what I had let happen to it.

The elevator bucked into motion. By then it was almost dark outside, the rain falling harder now, dimpling the sleek plastic cage around me. I looked up at the bright light in the top of the elevator. No need giving Nick another free shot while I was trapped in a five-by-five chic architectural coffin. I reloaded the .357 and fired into the circular fluorescent light fixture. Sparks and slivers of glass fell around me. Now, at least, Burnucci wasn't gonna have a spotlight to help him.

Just as I slipped a cartridge in to replace the one I'd fired at the light, I realized that my elevator was catching up with the other one. Their elevator had stopped at a floor below, and I was coming down on them from above. I wanted to be ready for a shot, but there was no way. Firing into that glass box could ricochet a bullet into Camille no matter how accurate I was, and I wasn't feeling accurate at all. Then, as my elevator came almost even with theirs, I could see them for the first time since we started down.

Burnucci had dropped the Uzi. He was struggling with Camille who was jammed up against the control panel. She had the PPK in both hands, trying to get it leveled on Nick somehow. He managed to get a hand loose, made a fist of it, and hit her. Hard. As she spun away from the control buttons, their elevator started down again.

Nick reached down for the PPK. I knew what he'd do with it. That cut my range of choices to zip. I fired a round high and prayed. Camille was on the floor of the car. That was as safe as she could be. My bullet blew out the whole side of my elevator car, and shattered a panel of Burnucci's car. I saw him grab his throat and, for just an instant, I thought I'd made the shot of my life.

No such luck. He was clawing shards of glass out of his neck and cheek as he spun around, coming up with the Uzi and leveling it right on me. Lord, cancel my season pass to Saints games. Give my opera tickets to Denise. Let Wes slip a twenty-dollar gold piece in my vest, just so folks will know I died standing pat.

Nowhere to run, no use to duck. Caught in that damned glass vault, I aimed as Burnucci did, knowing he was gonna send ten bullets my way for every one I got off toward him—if I managed more than one.

As I pulled the trigger, everything went into slow motion. It was as if I could see my shot moving like molasses down the side of a bottle. It was on target, but his finger had already closed on the trigger, and whether my shot killed him or not, the Honky Express was bearing down on me for one last run—at the speed of light.

So when that burst went upward, chewing the roof out of my elevator, I couldn't understand. Not till I looked back at Burnucci's crazed face and saw him jerking backward over and over again as if somebody had slipped a 220-volt wire up his pants leg and into his shorts. The Uzi fell from his hands, and he did this slow turn like a clumsy ballerina, turning and turning.

Until he was face to face with Camille whose eyes were on fire, whose bloodied lips were moving like coiled wire, who was screaming some single phrase at him each time she pulled the trigger of the PPK.

I could hear the silenced reports of the pistol one after another as Camille's shots ripped into Burnucci, as they tore him to pieces. I tried to yell at Camille to stop, to tell her that one was plenty, that I doctored the bullets in my hideout gun. They were 7.65mm wad-cutters with mercury fulminate in the slugs.

As I watched tranced, the unbroken panels of their elevator began to darken as if dusk was falling, not simply out in the world beyond, but especially in that elevator car as it drifted back down toward the earth below. It took eight years. That's how many rounds there were in the PPK clip and chamber. By the time the gun fell silent, I could barely see into the other elevator. A thick dark curtain of Burnucci's blood and flesh obscured everything.

But I could hear. I could hear Camille's voice. Not the voice of a terrified woman, but what those furies that followed Orestes must have sounded like: a voice from the depths of the world, from the rocks and plants, out of the heart of stars, from where things rise into life and wilt into death. The sound of a woman claiming her vengeance, and I never want to hear it again if I live a hundred years.

—Danny . . . my baby . . . Danny . . . my baby . . .

The lobby was empty. I knew it would be. In a hostage situation like this, they'd stay clear. Don't push a freak—until you can push him straight into hell. They were out there, though. Our Tactical people, our Quick Reaction people. Probably every off-duty cop in Orleans Parish and as many cowboys from the Jefferson Parish Sheriff's Office as had heard the police radio traffic in Orleans.

I came out of my elevator and stood in front of the one Camille was in, waiting for the door to open, with my Magnum poised and ready. Knowing there was no need at all.

But the doors didn't open. I pulled my stiletto from around my neck where it seemed I'd strung it years before and started prizing on the doors. They came easy, and I used both hands to shove them open. Then I stood back, looking into the elevator where Camille and Burnucci had come down.

The light inside had been knocked out by one shot or another, and Camille was backlit by the sodium lamps in the parking lot outside. She was sitting on the floor at the back of the car, arms folded, head down. I squinted into the darkness at floor level, because for a moment I couldn't see Burnucci. The floor was covered with what looked like old clothes soaked in oil. When I did manage to make him out, I wished I hadn't.

They say the first turn of the screw cancels all debts. Nick was paid off in full. Even Amadeo and his people couldn't wish more. I wondered if anyone in the coroner's office had ever run an autopsy on hamburger.

I picked Camille up in my arms, and bent down to find

the PPK in the shambles we were leaving behind. She whispered something to me that I couldn't make out.

—Are you all right, honey? Did he hurt you?

—Danny . . . my baby, was all she said.

They had taken Camille to the manager's suite, and I was drinking Bushmills out of a bottle Wes Colvin had scouted up somewhere and bleeding on the River Tower lobby sofa like a stuck hog. Mauvais was over at the elevator bank with somebody from the coroner's office. I think the ME was lodging a complaint or something. I didn't blame him. It's got to be beneath an MD's dignity to write up hash.

—Jesus, Wes was saying, —remember when the grain ship exploded down at the port? Guys they were pulling out of the hold looked better than . . .

I leaned back and took a giant swallow. I wasn't sure how long I'd been awake, but it wasn't gonna be much longer.

—Quit making so much of it. I saw a guy get it in the minefield east of the Berlin Wall. They left him there for three days. It was August . . . too early for the fall flowers, but . . . there was this sweet sickening smell like . . .

Wes was staring at me. I got quiet and took my third drink.

—You want to tell me off the record why . . . I mean, eight slugs?

—How could you tell?

—I couldn't. Nobody could. I heard a cop say that's what the Walther holds.

—Well . . .

—They weren't police issue, either. Explosive? Dum-dum?

—Would you ask Pollock how he mixes paint?

—If it blew a guy to pieces, yeah. Yeah, I think so.

—Wet trade, Wesley. Not like you country boys upstate with your hawglegs and bourbon and pickup trucks. Hard shit... you'll never know...

Mauvais was done with the ME, or maybe the ME was done with him. Somebody was snapping pictures of the inside of the elevator. That's when I figured out why Pollock had come to mind.

Before Mauvais could get to me, a corpsman appeared out of nowhere and started cutting away the right side of my coveralls. What with the left arm already gone, I considered I might have to go to the army surplus on Metairie Road and see what they had in stock.

—Wes, I said, —you want to catch this.

I believe he grabbed the bottle out of my hand just as I passed out.

When I woke up, I felt Camille's arms around me, her lips on my cheek. Mauvais was sitting opposite me, and the ambulance people were coming in with a gurney. Wes was sitting beside me, looking anxious.

—Get 'em out of here, I told Mauvais, waving my limp little wrist at the orderlies. —I walked in, and I'm gonna walk out.

Mauvais's eyes went hard. He motioned the stretcher-bearers away. —Okay, if you can walk out, you can talk. Let me hear it.

I took the bottle back from Wes. I didn't feel much in my side, but my goddamned shoulder was in terrible shape. That worried me. Sergeant Murray used to say you never felt the one that killed you. When he was bleeding to death in my arms, he told me the same thing. He wasn't feeling anything, and the rum and Coke tasted just fine.

—Listen, I whispered to Camille, —you go along with me on this, hear?

—What?

—Do it. For once in your life, just do what I say.

She backed off like I'd slapped her. I thought I better get into my number before I slipped away again.

—Gun's mine. Burnucci was bringing us down in the elevator. He looked away, and I came up with my hideout. Is there something else?

During the silence, I had me another snort from the Bushmills. Mauvais looked at me like I was crazy. Wes's expression would have fit better if he'd been staring into my coffin. Camille was frowning and about to say something. I cut her off.

—I think it would be real nice if somebody got this lady back to the hospital. She's been through a lot, and it's not done yet.

—I'll take her, Wes said quickly. He didn't know just what was going on, but he was trying to help the very best he could. —You want to come along?

—Colvin, Mauvais said, —you go on ahead with Mrs. Bynum. Captain Trapp is with me.

Wes wanted to answer back, but I frowned at him. If Mauvais wanted to drive me down to Sacre Coeur and piss and moan at me all the way down, it was all right. I'd made it past Boston Club, and I'd make it past him. In fact, I was determined to bleed all over his car. Maybe even throw up if I could.

But few things go the way you reckon. Mauvais put my arm over his shoulder and helped me stagger through the autumn rain to his car. I was surprised how strong the old man was. As he pulled out of the parking lot, I looked back at River Tower. If I ever move out of the Olympia Apartments, I thought, it won't be to there.

We drove back to Magazine Street before Mauvais said anything.

—You going to stay with your story? he asked almost casually.

—Why, Major, I...

—You've already got a board on Hawkins. You want one on why you emptied your gun into a suspect, blew him to pieces?

—Danny... my baby, I said beneath my breath.

—What?

—Nothing.

—Well?

—I was tired and hurt, Major. I lost it for a minute.

We drove another two blocks.

—All right, he said. —I'll see what I can do.

—Huh?

He looked over at me, and he was smiling. Not that little bullshit smile. The real thing.

—You weren't in that damned elevator. And you didn't blow Burnucci away.

I tried to play Man in the Iron Mask, but I know it slipped a little. Maybe I *was* gonna throw up, without even meaning to.

—Look, I was there, I said.

—Yeah. In the next elevator, shot up, trying to figure any way you could to...

He paused and pulled over to the side of the street.

—One thing...

—Sir?

—How the hell did you get that PPK to Mrs. Bynum?

—Uh, ah...

He reached into his glove compartment and pulled out a pint of rye. He took a whack and passed it over.

—In your condition, you might as well mix 'em. You've got nothing to lose.

—When I can't get Irish, I do rye, I said.

It damned near scorched my liver. They've gone light

on the Irish, but Old Overholt is still a killer. I hoped none of it leaked out my side.

—I skidded it into the elevator just as the sonofabitch shot me.

—And she did the rest?

—She's hurting enough. I'll swear to God I shot him, I said.

—Forget it. I got it right with the ME. Righteous shooting... multiple wounds. They don't pay him any extra to count them. I can't get you off a board of enquiry on the Hawkins thing. She was a police officer. But forget Burnucci. We're gonna scrape him up and flush him. He's not worth a board.

He started up the car again, and I caught a glimpse at him out of the corner of my eye. He was smiling, feeling good. It made me feel better. Maybe the old man was all right. Maybe we both were.

—You said she's going to lose her boy? he asked as we pulled into the emergency entrance at Sacre Coeur.

—Yeah, I told him. —She's already lost him. Now she's looking for the strength to let him go.

Mauvais helped me into the ER and set me down. We shook hands just like it was the most ordinary thing.

—I don't blame you, he was saying. —I don't blame you for any of it. You've got a bad mouth and the worst style I ever came across, but...

—Remember Sergeant Murray? I asked him.

—Of course. That old redneck bastard. He called me spook and jive-ass. Said I'd never get past probation.

His voice trailed off. He knew Sergeant Murray, all right.

—And he made me a cop, Mauvais said at last.

—That's two of us, I told him as the orderlies came to take me away.

—I'll speak to your friend in the DA's office. If Denise

Lemoyne will go along with me, there won't be any grand jury on this one.

As some ER people began fussing over me, Mauvais back away. —Give Mrs. Bynum my best, he said.

—That is your best, Major, I heard myself saying as they stretched me on a table and started cutting my damned coveralls all to pieces again.

CHAPTER
15

When I awoke, I remembered everything. I came up in my bed like somebody was still shooting at me. I wished I hadn't. It felt like I'd been on the underside of a stampede. If it didn't hurt, it's 'cause I didn't have one. They told me I'd slept the night through and the day around. I told them it wasn't long enough.

Sister Mary Cecilia came in smiling, whomping up my pillow, feeling my forehead. If they had a contest between her and a digital thermometer, my money's on the nun.

—You're quite a celebrity, she told me brightly.

—The word's "survivor," Sister.

She nodded, her smile still in place. —That, too. I'm glad you came through, Ralph. But I wish you'd be more careful.

—Jesus ... I mean, gee, Sister, you wouldn't believe how careful I am. If I wasn't ...

She stood silent for a moment. There was a question she wanted to ask, but she wasn't going to put it on me unless I wanted her to.

—Okay, Sister. Shoot. I mean, was there something?

She shook her head and looked like a little girl who wanted to ask "Why?"

—You work out there in the streets. All I see here is ... the result. But ... how could a man kill his own father?

—And his own son, I said. —I guess Nick had to believe there's something better than a father ... or a son. Something a man could want so much, he'd ...

Sister Mary Cecilia bit her lip and looked down. —Poor Dominic. I'll remember him in my ...

—Forget it, Sister. Pray for Nick, and the saints will laugh at you. Pray for the old man. Franco was okay ... in his way.

—You think so?

—It was a bad way, but he cared about his family.

When Wes came in, he had my sports bag in his hand.

—I rummaged through your place while you were out, he grinned. —Under the grenades and claymores and boxes of ammo, I found some clothes.

—Where's my coveralls?

—I think they threw them in the bag with Burnucci.

—I had them things in Germany, I told him. —They were good luck.

Wes nodded and tossed a fresh copy of the *Item* on my bed. There was a picture of me from about ten years ago. I was looking like the hardnose I'd been back then. They had separate articles on Franco's death and the shoot-out at River Tower. Nothing on Nick's connection to Danny. Then a small piece at the bottom of the page caught my eye.

Mauvais had put out a press release saying Max Hawkins had died in the line of duty trying to make a narcotics arrest in Desire project. He hadn't told me he was gonna do that. Maybe he didn't think he had to. He was right.

Wes was looking pleased with himself.

—Nice, huh?

—Fucking journalistic connivance in a departmental whitewash.

—Yeah. Nice, huh?

—It *is* nice. For me as much as for her.

—Denise and Mauvais got together. They worked over the reports. Denise signed your name to the new copies. Mauvais shredded the originals.

—Jesus, they ought to write novels together.

—They wanted to make it come out right.

—Like I say, fiction's their thing.

Wes held out a handful of electric wiring. —I took all the stuff from your coveralls back to your place. Except for these. What the hell were you going to do with a bunch of wire?

I laughed and took the ignition wires out of his hand.

—I already did it, I told him. —I short-circuited the Honky Express.

When Wes was gone, I eased into the clothes he'd brought me. When I buttoned my shirt over the cracked ribs, I wished I had less vanity. The damned thing was tailored to my best weight, and my right side was swollen a couple of sizes.

Only in New Orleans, I was thinking. Only down here at the ass-end of the Mississippi would people junk the truth, step on it, shred it, so that a girl who wanted out of the projects bad enough to kill could go to her grave with a good name. Shit, what do I know? Maybe truth is overrated. Maybe being kind to people now and then is worth more than truth. I don't believe it, but I'm not gonna knock folks who do. I made a note to think more about it the next time I was able to run in Audubon Park.

•   •   •

It was evening then, and I figured Sister Mary Cecilia had gone off duty. Maybe I could slip down to Camille's room and see how she was doing. Walking was a bitch, but I'd been hurt worse and still stayed in motion.

I practiced by going up to the fourth floor in the elevator and walking down to the waiting room. There was a big picture window looking out to the west. The clouds had parted, and the sun was almost touching the horizon.

It would still be bright afternoon in California. If Danny Bynum and his momma had stayed out there, it would have been better. He shouldn't have come so far looking for a man he didn't know.

As I watched, the sun began to lose itself, settling down below the edge of the world. It made me want to wish for something, but there was nothing left to wish for. Everything was settled now, like the sun. Tomorrow it would start again, but I was too smart to let myself think of that.

Then I recalled it wasn't quite all done. As the light started to die and the autumn darkness began covering the cars and people in the streets down below, I remembered Camille had one thing left to do. I thought maybe it would be easier—no, at least possible—for her if she had someone from the old times, from the project, beside her. Someone who could scream without making a sound.

She was wearing a long white robe, sitting at the table in the dark, looking out into the fall evening just as I had been doing down the hall a few minutes before. The truth of it was I hadn't wanted to come to be with her now. I wanted to call Denise and Wes and invite them to supper. I wanted to celebrate passing under the gun once more, just being alive when I had no business being. I wanted to laugh till my side and shoulder hurt, and drink good liquor and plan a fishing trip to the Gulf Coast. But I was here, thinking what to say, wondering when the dark ceremonies would begin.

She heard me, called softly for me to join her. I could see her profile against the faint last light from outside. It seemed I could remember her sitting on a stoop at Desire, her face thrust up toward the emerging stars, telling me what she wanted to do and be, the places she meant to see, how she was going to spend her life, while out in the grassy court kids ran and played and chased one another, and I could hear my mother singing in the kitchen a couple of doors down.

I knew it wasn't a single time I was remembering, but time after time. My only mistake had been thinking we'd be doing and seeing and spending all of our time together. No, not my only mistake. Just the one that had hurt worst.

But that had been long ago, in another country where black people's dreams, no matter how small, had a way of falling apart—unless the people had some special quality: toughness like mine, beauty like hers.

With evening shadows conspiring to soften the years, it seemed Camille hadn't changed at all. She was still beautiful. I felt my breath catch in my throat and realized why I really hadn't wanted to come. When she started to speak, I could hardly hear her. She wasn't telling me her dreams now. She was summing up her nightmares.

—If I'd never set foot in that car of his...

—That's going back pretty far, isn't it?

—Just far enough. You and I... we would have made it together, wouldn't we?

—I like to think so, I said. —I like it so much I used to think about it all the time.

—I thought it was for my baby, she almost whispered.

—Lord, I thought, not in Desire, not in the projects at all. I wanted a life for him, but I gave him death.

—No, I said, —Nick Burnucci did that. Danny's father did that.

Camille turned to me for the first time. Her eyes were dark, hollow. While I'd been sleeping she'd been wide awake, doing penance, I thought, for other people's sins.

—I shouldn't have told Nick that Danny was his son, she said, her voice rising, almost conversational now. —He believed me in 1965, and he still believed it when he...

I heard what she said clearly enough. I just couldn't make sense of it.

—What are you saying, Camille? If Nick wasn't...

She stood up, looking in her white robe like some ghostly priestess, and walked toward Danny's room. I followed, listening. She stopped at the door.

—I was pregnant before I met Nick Burnucci, she said. —Danny made me tell him the truth. That's why he put New Orleans on the tour.

—Burnucci thought Danny was going to claim...

—I guess he did, but Nick didn't have to worry. He didn't have to kill his father. He didn't have to kill... my baby. Danny wasn't his.

Danny knew that? But...

—Danny sent you that concert ticket. He didn't tell me, but I knew. I knew when I heard the way he sang that first song of his. After the concert, he was going to...

I understood what she was saying, and I knew it was true. Not because of what she said or even how she said it, her eyes locked on mine, her lips scarcely moving, telling me a truth twenty years too late. I just knew.

—Oh, Jesus, I heard myself cry out. Not loud, but not silent either. —Oh, sweet Lord...

I turned away from her, gain and loss jumbled and fused in my mind. But when I turned, I was facing into the shadowed room suffused with blue light, banks of

humming machinery around the bed, each one register-
ing with lights or oscilloscopes or digital read-outs the
same sorry message over and over again. Nothing. Nothing. Nothing.

I didn't turn again. I walked to the side of the bed and
looked down at my son who lay dreaming in a sleep that
would last forever. His face was untroubled. I think his
long lashes fluttered on his cheeks. Or maybe it was nothing but the shaking of my hands on the bedrails.

Behind me, like a chorus, Camille was still talking. Not
to me, not even to our boy, but to whatever there is behind
the scenery of the world that hears the tragic chorus and
is moved or unmoved by it.

—It was the only way I knew. Like I was lost in the
sea, and a boat came by, and I grabbed hold and Nick
pulled me in. I told myself, All I have to do is this, and
my baby will be shut of Desire . . . because even a gangster
couldn't send his own back to that . . . Could he?

No. He could do worse. No. Not worse. The same,
only quicker. I didn't even want to raise Burnucci from
the dead, reassemble the rubbish Camille had reduced
him to, so that I could kill him again. I didn't even think
of him. It was worse than that.

I saw twenty years of a child's growing, Christmases
and birthdays, bicycles and a first guitar, arguments and
pain that was all right because it was between the three
of us. It was me who had churned the Milky Way, but I
hadn't drawn him in from the sea.

In the silence beyond his bed I could hear the machinery
breathing and stuttering. The displays winked like stars
in the darkness there. Then I heard a sound I recognized,
a long low moan of anguish and triumph and loss exactly
like the one that Danny had used to start his song.

It was coming from me.

·   ·   ·

We passed the night there together, the three of us, Camille and I as silent as Danny. We held his hands and blamed no one, not even Burnucci, for what had befallen us. It was too deep, too impenetrable and ruinous for a man in a white Cadillac or a System or even Desire to have brought upon us. Better we take the thing on ourselves: her for thinking there could be any way out we didn't make for ourselves; me for walking away and fighting strangers in alleys four thousand miles away instead of finding Burnucci, tearing him apart, and taking my woman home.

When the sky began to lighten, I phoned downstairs. In a little while, Dick Lanier came up. I looked at Camille, and then I nodded to him. He walked over to the machines.

—Wait a minute, I managed to choke out. —Show me how. I was in at the creation...

He showed me what had to be done, and in two or three minutes it was over. I could hardly tell the difference, but there was one. It was dawn and the room was filling with sunlight when I leaned down over Danny to say good-bye. I wished it hadn't been the first time I kissed him.

That afternoon, I walked Camille down the concourse at New Orleans International to a private gate where a chartered plane was waiting. A silent horde of fans wearing white headbands had been left behind at the security check. The four remaining members of Desire Project preceded us. They were taking Danny back to California. He'd been happy there. It was where he'd found the music and the words to the only song he really wanted to sing. They'd be in Los Angeles before night came again.

I guess Camille was past tears, or maybe what we had

learned in Desire wasn't gone, flushed out of our souls. Only put aside for a little while.

—It's like it never happened, she said dreamily. —We're standing here together. Danny's gone, Nick dead. I think I dreamed it all.

—No, I said. —You lived it. I was the one dreaming.

She put her arms around me and we kissed. Not a kiss of sympathy or shared pain. Or even a good-bye.

—Will you be staying in L.A.? I asked.

She shook her head. —No, she said. —I don't think so. This is my home ... isn't it?

I nodded and held her close. —Whenever you're ready. Are you sure you don't want me to come?

—No, it ... doesn't matter, she said almost brightly. —You and Danny ... met. That's what he wanted.

She was gone then, striding out to the private jet where the rest of the boys who had made up Desire Project were waiting for her, sons to comfort a mother for a brother lost. She walked with her head held high, shoulders back, looking like a twenty-year-old girl who was already living in a future she was determined to make. For herself. Maybe she would. And maybe, as she boarded the plane for her flight toward the sun, she was hearing in her mind and her heart the same words as me.

... I wanna be a wise child too ...